Acidic Fiction

Acidic Fiction #2

Toxic Tales

Edited by Steven x Davis

The stories in this book were originally published between
January 1, 2015 and June 30, 2015 on www.acidicfiction.com.

Foreword © 2015 Steven x Davis
Stories © 2015 their respective authors
Cover design by Mark Davis

ISBN-10: 0-692-53738-4
ISBN-13: 978-0-692-53738-1

Creation is an act of sheer will. Next time, it'll be flawless.

– John Hammond, *Jurassic Park*

Table of Contents

Foreword
The Death of a Magazine

In the future, it will be difficult for me to describe *Acidic Fiction* as anything but a failed endeavor. It's not because I failed at what I set out to do, which was to improve on the flawed submission processes of other magazines, read and publish excellent stories, pay their authors, and showcase an underrepresented genre of fiction. I think I managed to do all those things to the best of my ability.

On the other hand, I failed to properly promote the magazine and its authors, establish a presence in the speculative fiction community, raise funds, or do any of the many other things that are necessary for the long-term survival of an online magazine. For those reasons, among others, the failure of the site was inevitable.

When I started the site, I didn't have anything close to a long-term plan, just the basic goals I listed above. On a personal level, I also wanted to hone my skills as an editor and explore the current climate of speculative fiction. I hoped that *Acidic Fiction* would bring in some money eventually, but I set aside an initial investment for the site knowing I would probably never recoup it. I did almost all the work myself, putting my many eclectic skills to use and picking up a few more along the way.

After I published the first anthology, I found myself at a crossroads. My funds were starting to dwindle and I doubted that anthology sales would bring in enough money to keep the site going. I had to decide between setting aside more of my own money to pay for new stories, significantly cutting the pay rates for authors, or ending the magazine when the money ran out.

In addition to the financial aspect, I also had to acknowledge that I was spending an inordinate amount of time on *Acidic Fiction* and very little on my own writing or other paying projects.

If I had redoubled my efforts and re-invested in the magazine, there was a slight chance it could have been successful eventually. There were many things I hadn't tried yet, and I was still receiving and publishing plenty of high-quality stories. I always knew the project had potential, but I wasn't sure if I could properly explore it.

The question was this: Did I want *Acidic Fiction* to be the primary focus of my career, or did I want to spend my time, money, and effort elsewhere? After some deliberation, I decided that I should publish the stories I had already purchased and wrap up the project with this second anthology.

Before I finally move on, I wanted to make a few last remarks.

While the magazine was active, I read more than 1,100 short story submissions and ultimately published 74 stories on the site. Of those, I reprinted 28 in the two *Acidic Fiction* anthologies: *Corrosive Chronicles* and *Toxic Tales*.

Although I did enjoy reading many of those submissions, going through them was the most arduous part of the job. A frustrating number did not meet the submission guidelines, several needed substantial revision before any editor could even consider them, and a few were practically unintelligible. Despite the difficulty of that effort, I still believe it was worthwhile to respond to each of those submissions.

Due to some poor planning on my part, I was forced to publish one of my own short stories to fill an unexpectedly empty slot in the second week of the magazine's existence. I published it under a pseudonym (James Essex) because I didn't want to come across as vain or incompetent, although I probably deserved both labels. That particular story, "Medication," received the fewest hits of any story on the site, which certainly kept my vanity in check. Naturally, my

Foreword

incompetence has never been called into question.

After I chose to end the magazine, I published one last story under my own name ("Leap into the Sky") because I felt like I should go down with the ship. I'd like to think that I would still have published that story if it had been written by someone else, but of course it's impossible to properly distance myself from my own work.

Regardless of its objective merit, I did not reprint my story in this book because I wanted to focus on other authors.

In fact, the primary reason I chose to publish another anthology was to expose the best stories from *Acidic Fiction* to a larger audience. Whether or not this book finds that audience, I think it will be a pleasant surprise to anyone who takes a chance and reads it.

Hopefully all of these authors will continue to be published in much more successful magazines with many more readers. In the meantime, this book will have to do.

For what it's worth, I still think that speculative fiction in a contemporary setting is a genre with limitless potential, and I hope it continues to be explored even more than it has been in *Acidic Fiction*.

When I read stories like the one in this book, I remember that I did accomplish what I set out to do after all.

And it was a smashing success.

Thank you very much for reading.

Steven x Davis
Former Editor-in-chief, *Acidic Fiction*

Faceless

by M. B. Vujačić

Don't smoke while walking.

That's what Irma's mother had said whenever she saw Irma and her friends strolling around the neighborhood with cigarettes in their hands. Apparently, smoking while walking caused you to inhale more of the cancerous stuff than if you were sitting or lying down. And boy oh boy, did it piss Irma off every time she felt like lighting up while on the move.

Like now. It was nine in the evening and still 90 degrees with no wind. She was on her way home from work, every inch of her body clammy from standing all day in a clothing store—one that didn't allow its employees to smoke, not even in the bathroom—and she couldn't enjoy a goddamn cigarette without being haunted by some factoid her mother had read in a magazine 20 years ago.

"Christ," she said, lighting the cigarette.

The first few drags tasted like heaven, but then she started getting an itch in her throat. Constantly talking to customers had left her mouth feeling as dry as emery.

There was no one at the bus stop. She sat on the bench and took her battered old flip phone from her purse. She'd just started texting Jake to let him know she'd be home soon, when a car came screeching from a nearby intersection. It was black and looked like a sports car, only bulkier. Its driver gave exactly zero fucks about traffic rules, cutting diagonally across the street. Horns shrieked as the cars in the opposite lane swerved out of its path. It headed straight toward the bus stop.

"Jesus Christ!" Irma shouted, scrambling away from the bench.

The car veered left with another screech, careened onto the sidewalk, and lurched to a stop just short of a wall. The driver's door opened and a man stepped out. He wore a gray fedora and a leather trench coat so long it resembled a robe. Deep shadows covered his features, making him look as if he didn't have a face at all.

"The Hell you think you're doing, you goddamn idiot?" Irma screamed at him.

Mr. Faceless ignored her. He slammed the door and strode into the building he'd almost crashed into. He passed under a streetlamp, yet somehow his head remained in total darkness. As he raised his hand to ring the intercom, she saw that he was wearing leather gloves.

He held the button for a full minute. When nobody answered, he grabbed the door and pushed. It flew open with a *clang*, making Irma flinch. He went inside.

Slowly, ready to back off quickly if he returned, Irma approached Mr. Faceless's car. It wasn't a sports car. Hell, it wasn't anything. No manufacturer logo, no model name, no license plate, nothing to indicate where it came from. Which was weird, since it looked expensive. Maybe it was custom made.

She noticed that Mr. Faceless had forgotten to close the driver side window. She glanced at the building he'd entered, then looked into the car. Its interior was all leather, chrome, and fancy touchscreens. A bobblehead cat stood on the dashboard. It wore a garish suit, its huge head dominated by big bloodshot eyes and a tiny grinning mouth full of rotten teeth. A smartphone lay on the passenger seat.

Irma took another glance at the building Mr. Faceless had disappeared into, then returned her attention to the smartphone. She'd never owned a touchscreen phone, but Jake had one, and the way it could play movies and browse funny-picture websites had always made her want one, too. Also, she wanted to get back at Mr. Faceless for almost running her over.

Faceless

A bus appeared at the end of the street. Irma watched it draw closer until she made sure it was the one she was waiting for, and thought, *Ah, Hell. Now or never.* She leaned into the car, took the smartphone, and stuffed it into her purse, then she got on the bus. The doors rattled to a close as it started moving. Irma smiled.

A perfect crime.

♦

She found Jake on the living room couch, munching popcorn and watching a reality show. He was a wiry, tattooed guy with a mullet and a Fu Manchu mustache. Irma had met him a couple years earlier, after his ex-wife left him and took their kids. He wasn't much of a provider, but at least he didn't mind the stretch marks under her arms or the ever-increasing size of her ass.

"Hey, babe," he said. "Want some popcorn?"

"No, thanks." Irma took the smartphone from her purse and placed it on the coffee table.

"What's that?"

She smiled. "I picked it up."

He took the smartphone. "You bought it?"

"Nope. Some rich guy left a window open on his sports car and it was inside." She shrugged.

Jake chuckled. "Did you turn it off?"

"Dunno how."

He looked the phone over. "Where's the off button on this thing?"

Irma shrugged again and went into the kitchen to make coffee. She was reaching for the sugar when a sound like a dozen out-of-tune pipe organs shrieking in unison boomed from the living room. It startled her so badly she almost dropped the sugar bowl.

"Jesus Christ, Jake, turn the TV down!"

"It's not the TV. It's this phone!"

"What? Seriously?"

She came back to the living room. The phone was lying on the coffee table, its display shining with a toxic green light, ringing so loud it drowned out the TV. Jake sat with his arms crossed, staring at it.

"What are we gonna do?" Irma shouted over the noise.

"Nothing. Just wait for it to stop."

"Can't you turn the sound off?"

He shook his head. "It doesn't have volume buttons and I dunno how to unlock it. Must be some new software or something."

Irma had no idea what he was talking about and didn't care. She sat next to him and they stared at the phone together. When it didn't stop ringing for a full minute, she dropped it on the couch and pressed a pillow over it. No use. After another five minutes of the cacophony, she found herself seriously thinking of taking a hammer to the damn thing.

"Oh, to Hell with this," Irma said. She took the smartphone and tapped the ANSWER CALL icon. When it finally went quiet, she pressed it against her ear. "Yeah?"

"I want my phone back," a man said. His voice sounded wet and guttural, like it came from his stomach instead of his lungs.

"And I want a million bucks."

"I need my phone and I need it *now*."

"Buy another one with your platinum card. I'm sure you won't even notice."

"I had a very bad day. Do *not* make me come there."

"You a cop?"

He chuckled. It sounded like his throat was full of slime. "Of course not."

"Then fuck you," Irma said, hanging up.

"He'll call again," Jake said.

She lit a cigarette. "Good. Maybe the battery will run out." She put the ashtray in her lap and leaned back.

They sat in silence for a while, waiting for the smartphone to ring again. It didn't.

Jake kept fidgeting with it for an hour before giving up. He couldn't even figure out what brand it was, let alone how to unlock it or remove the SIM card. "Made in Abberon" was etched on its side, but whether that was a city, a factory, or a third-world country, the two of them had no idea.

"I'll take it to Fred tomorrow," Irma said after they went to bed. "He sells these things; he'll know what it is. Maybe I can get a few hundred bucks for it."

Jake kissed her, his hand cupping her breast. "My criminal mastermind."

"Yeah, I should change my name to Soprano or something."

♦

Irma yawned.

It was noon, hot as the Devil's armpit, and she was at the sales counter. She'd received a call from her boss around seven in the morning. He had told her his allergies were acting up again and asked if she wouldn't mind taking the morning shift. She'd groaned inwardly but agreed anyway.

So there she was, trying to act interested while a shriveled housewife complained how today's fashion industry manipulated women into spending more money by promoting layered clothing and making every new garment thinner than the last. The woman had just begun elaborating on the benefits of cotton over synthetic when Irma's flip phone started ringing.

Irma glanced at it, saw "JAKE calling" on the screen, and pressed the Silent Mode button. The ringing stopped, but she could still hear it vibrating and it made her want to throw it at a wall.

"Sorry," she said. "You were saying?"

After the housewife left, Irma went to the counter and took out her cell phone. Two missed calls, both from Jake. She exhaled loudly and dialed his number. It rang three times before he picked up.

"Why are you calling me at work, you moron?" she said, "I told you to—"

"Where is my phone?"

For a moment, Irma just stood there, leaning on the counter, wondering if she'd called the wrong number. Then she recognized that deep, gargling voice and the way it somehow made the words sound sticky and viscous, and just like that, her heart started beating so loud she could hardly hear her thoughts.

"Where is my phone?" Mr. Faceless repeated. "Did you hide it?"

"W-where's Jake?"

"He is here."

"Is ... is he okay?"

"Never better. I want my phone. Did you take it to work with you?"

Irma put a hand over her mouth.

"I can find it myself, you know. I can follow its smell," he said. "But then I would have to find *you* first."

"P-put Jake on the phone."

Mr. Faceless let out a "heh" that sounded like he had loose gravel under his tongue. "Irma wants to talk to you."

She heard some rustling, and then Jake said. "B-babe? That you?" His speech was slurred, as if he'd suffered a stroke.

"Jake, you okay?"

"Babe, he's a ... like a shadow ... he broke the door with his—" Jake coughed, wheezing like an asthmatic. "Babe ... oh my God, he ... he has so many eyes."

"Jake, I—"

She heard more rustling, and then Mr. Faceless said, "Come home.

We will be waiting."

"I-I'll be there in half an—"

"I hear sirens. One of your neighbors must have called the police." He snorted. "Nothing can ever be simple, now can it?"

There was a click as the line went dead.

Irma picked up her purse and rushed out. She crossed a dozen yards before realizing she'd forgotten to close the store. She went back, locked up, and almost left the key in the door. She dialed Jake's number again as she walked toward the bus station, only to have a robotic voice tell her the number was unavailable.

Mr. Faceless was right; Irma had taken his smartphone to the store with her. She'd planned to drop by Fred's house after work so he could look at it and tell her how much she could get for it.

Now she took it out of her purse and pressed it against her chest. She hadn't prayed since she was a kid, but she prayed now. Prayed that, at any moment, the smartphone would ring and that Jake would be the one calling.

But it didn't. Not even a peep.

♦

Jake was dead.

Irma knew it the moment she saw the ambulance and police cars in front of her apartment building. She knew it because their lights were flashing but their sirens were quiet.

As she came closer, she saw other details that made her want to shriek: a cop telling a bunch of kids there was nothing to see, another cop leaning against a tree and trying not to retch, and a paramedic standing in the shade with a cigarette in hand, his face unreadable.

A cop stopped her at the entrance, asking where she was headed. Irma had to repeat the number of her apartment three times before she managed to say it loud enough for him to hear. He swallowed and explained her apartment was now a crime scene. She couldn't go inside until the detectives and forensic technicians had examined it. It wasn't until she asked if he'd seen Jake that she noticed how pale he looked. Yes, he told her, he'd seen him, and it would be better for her if she didn't.

For hours after that, Irma saw everything as if through a glazed lens. More people showed up—cops mostly, but there was also a group of men and women equipped with metal briefcases and clad in what appeared to be blue raincoats. They all went into the building and stayed there for a long time. She kept expecting them to come out carrying a large black bag with a zipper running up its length. Instead, they brought out a bunch of smaller white bags, many no bigger than the ones she stored frozen meat in.

Two men in suits approached her. They introduced themselves, though she instantly forgot their names, and told her they were detectives. Their faces differed—one was covered in wrinkles and had big rabbit teeth, the other was boyish with sleepy, gray eyes—but their voices sounded exactly the same, soft, slow, and sensitive in a way that made them easy to talk to. When they asked if Jake had any enemies, Irma told them she knew who the killer was.

They took her to the station, sat her down at a table with a camera pointing at her face, brought her an ashtray and a glass of water, and listened to her statement.

When she told them how Mr. Faceless had driven like a maniac before entering a building next to the bus stop, the younger detective inclined his head and asked if she could name the street where it happened. Their expressions didn't change after she gave them the address, but they began leaning closer, asking if she could remember the number of the building and the exact time of day. When she asked, "Why? What did he do there?" they apologized and explained that they weren't at liberty to discuss ongoing cases.

Irma described Mr. Faceless's car in as much detail as she could remember, up to and including the bobblehead cat. She didn't mention the smartphone, though. She had different plans for it. Instead, she told them Mr. Faceless called her at home and threatened to hurt her for "insulting his driving." She swore she had no idea how he'd gotten her number, let alone her address.

Later, the detectives brought in two of their colleagues and asked if she could repeat her story for them. When Irma finished talking, all four detectives went out. The younger one returned half an hour later. He told her they'd arranged for her to stay at a safe house for a few days. The police officers assigned to take her there were waiting outside.

"Can't I go to my place?"

He shook his head. "That wouldn't be wise."

"Are your people still there?"

"No, but depending on the lab and autopsy results, they may need to go back. We can't risk contaminating the crime scene."

"Please … I just need to pick up some clothes."

He sighed and said, "Wait here," then walked out, shutting the door.

He returned 10 minutes later. "You can make a quick stop at your apartment. The officers will escort you and tell you what to do. The kitchen and the living room are off limits. Is that alright?"

"Yeah. Thank you."

As the detective turned to leave, Irma said: "Wait … what did he do in that building?"

The detective paused, his jaw tightening. "Believe me, you really don't want to know."

♦

It's as if nothing happened, Irma thought.

She stood in the hallway, staring at the yellow tape crisscrossing the doorway of her home. The door was cracked around the knob; the lock looked like someone had taken a sledgehammer to it. Aside from that, everything was the same: the cold floor, the grinding of the elevators, the grandmas on the balconies, the neighbors walking their dogs. It was all business as usual. It made her feel like she was drowning.

One of the cops, his nametag identifying him as A. SMITH, gave the tape a little tug and said, "We'll have to duck under it, miss."

He had a big, flabby face and a bigger, flabbier neck that looked like it was about to spill over his collar. He waited until Irma gave a weak nod, then pushed the door open and somehow squeezed his bulk into the apartment without ripping the tape. He waved for her to come in. She swiped a lock of hair from her eye and followed. The other cop, J. MILES, came in after her.

The door that led into the living room stood wide open, giving her a good view of the shattered TV and the overturned coffee table, not to mention the red streaks on the walls and the stains on the carpet. The light was on, too. It might have been her imagination, but the shadows seemed ... odd, especially the large one behind the TV. It seemed deeper than the rest and lacked a recognizable shape. It also appeared to be moving slightly, as if—

Smith flipped the switch, plunging the living room into darkness. "Sorry, you weren't supposed to see that," he said. "They must've forgotten to turn off the lights."

It's okay, Irma thought. Or perhaps she'd said it out loud. She wasn't sure which.

"Please pack your things," Miles said.

Irma went into the bedroom and just stood there, staring at the bed. The sheets were still ruffled from the previous night, and strands of Jake's hair were still lying on his pillow. Everything looked the same as it did before she had left for work in the morning.

As a kid, Irma had loved watching action flicks where the hero went on a murderous rampage against the people who had harmed someone dear to him. The idea of exacting one's own justice sat well with her, which was why she'd been doing it her whole life, starting with the day she avenged the dolls her brother had broken by melting his plastic army men on the stove. It was the way she was made. Her gut reaction to being wronged would always be to claim an eye for an eye.

Or so she had thought. Mr. Faceless had wronged her more deeply than anyone else ever had, yet all she could do was stand here, an observer in her own head, not caring if they caught him or if he drove away laughing, just as long as he left her alone.

So she took his smartphone from her purse and dropped it on the bed, hoping it would be enough.

"Miss, can you hurry, please?"

"I, uh … just a minute."

Irma took her travel bag and opened the closet. She thought about asking Smith what sort of clothes she'd need in the safe house, then decided to just take whatever was clean. She began digging through her shirts when she chanced upon a shoe. It was made of some rough, black material, like a beetle's shell. Its twin lay even deeper in the closet, shoved under an old sweater. She'd never seen these shoes before, and had no idea what they were doing in there.

Irma was wondering whether she should tell the cops about this, when a glimmer from behind one of Jake's jackets caught her eye. She pushed the jacket aside and found herself staring at a leather trench coat so long its hem would drag on the floor if she tried to wear it. Underneath it, laid neatly down, sat a gray fedora.

Irma still stood there, the temperature in her guts rapidly changing from hot to cool to ice cold, when Smith screamed, "Jesus Christ!"

She heard the metallic click of a gun being cocked, followed by a gasp and a noise like something viscous being sucked through a straw. She rushed out of the bedroom and stopped in the doorway. Her mouth went slack.

The light in the living room was back on. The shadow—the big one from behind the TV—had moved from the wall to the hallway. It floated in midair, a flowing mass of darkness like a squid's ink cloud, its tendrils slithering into Mile's and Smith's ears and mouths and nostrils. Their knees were bent, arms hanging by their sides, eyes weeping black pus. They stood like that for a few moments, and then a scraping, ripping sound echoed from within them and they collapsed.

Irma watched the darkness flow toward her, unaware that she was backing away, until her legs struck the edge of the bed. She lost her balance and sat on the sheets, breathing in gasps so shallow she almost choked. She couldn't look away from the darkness, couldn't stop trying to figure out how it could fill the doorway and still be razor thin, and the more she tried, the more her brain felt hot, too hot, like it was boiling, like the sight of it stretched her sanity thin, way too thin, and—

"You have no idea how much trouble you put me in," it said.

—and she knew that voice dear God she recognized it and oh God help her he was like a fissure in reality and he had a head and it wasn't faceless it wasn't faceless at all because he grinned and laughed and then Irma too grinned and laughed **laughed LAUGHED** until Mr. Faceless said, "Yeah, I've always been a funny guy," and reached for her eyes.

Irma's scream could be heard half a block away.

♦

Mr. Faceless stepped from the bed and went to the closet.

He donned his clothes, taking care not to get any blood on his hat, then picked up his smartphone from where it lay among Irma's remains. It was splattered with blood and other fluids, but otherwise undamaged, thank God. He found a clean spot on the sheets and wiped the phone with it.

Mr. Faceless took a deep breath, counted to 10, and unlocked the display. No missed calls. Good. A dozen or so texts, each angrier than the last. Bad. Very, very bad.

He took another deep breath and tapped the topmost name in the contacts list. He pressed the smartphone against the side of what passed for his head, and waited. He hoped she wouldn't pick up. Then he heard a click and the ringing was replaced by her voice.

"Hey, you won't believe what happened," he said, "some lowlife stole my phone. Yeah, I left it in the car and forgot to close the window. ... Uh-huh, that's why I'm late, I had to track it down. ... No, I am not lying; I told you, someone *stole my phone*. If I was lying, don't you think I would have come up with a better sto— ... No, dammit, I didn't meet *her* again; I was tracking down my goddamn *phone*. Why do you always—" He leaned against the wall, shaking his head. "I *am* telling you the truth! ... Alright, we'll talk when I get home, do you— ... Sure, I'll buy some. ... Yes, don't worry, I—"

The line went dead.

Mr. Faceless stared at the smartphone for a few seconds, then sighed and let his hand drop to his side. He looked at what was left of Irma, and said, "Now look what you did."

Mr. Faceless left the apartment and pushed the elevator button, then decided to take the stairs anyway.

The night was dry and windless, the street deserted even though someone must have notified the police by now. It almost seemed like everyone had gone on a vacation. Everyone except him. Hell, he couldn't remember the last time he'd taken a day off. And where the Hell was he going to find fresh milk at this hour?

"What a time to be alive," he said, walking toward his car.

Crescent Cross
by Robert Luke Wilkins

Walter awoke to the sound of his wife Jessica throwing up in the adjacent bathroom. It happened every morning, a gift of her relentless morning sickness.

He stood, walked to the balcony door, and looked out. The view was spectacular. Their home was nestled against the side of a mountain, and the balcony faced southwest, perfect for sunsets, and the sun wouldn't blind you awake in the morning. You could leave the curtains and doors open on hot summer nights, and Crescent Cross had plenty of those.

Walter loathed the view.

He heard something smash downstairs, followed by the keening wail of a child. That was Michael. Walter had heard about The Terrible Twos, of course, but had never considered just how terrible they'd be once Michael escaped his crib.

"I'll deal with him," he called to his wife. He heard her retch and throw up again. He sighed.

If only they'd known.

Michael had smashed a vase and cut his arm in the process. It wasn't the first time, but Walter had thought this vase was out of the horror's reach. He should have known better. Michael's scope for havoc grew with every passing day.

"You're a devil," he said as he applied ointment to the cut. Michael only cried harder. He didn't really need to bother; he'd done this half a dozen times now, and every cut healed beautifully, without even a hint of a scar. But his habits wouldn't die.

Besides, with any luck, it wouldn't be for much longer. A man was coming to town today, and Walter was hoping to persuade him to buy their house.

The trouble was, he wasn't the only one selling.

♦

"It's a beautiful place," said the visitor, who had introduced himself as Jeremy Scott. "Are you the McAllisters?"

"That's us," said Walter with a smile, tapping the wooden nameplate on the fence. "A man in town makes the signs, and he gives discounts to new residents."

Jeremy nodded. "It's hard to find towns like this now," he said. "One that really has that small town *feel*. Honestly, I can't imagine why you'd want to move away."

"Work," Walter lied. "It's too far to commute, and I just can't afford to be picky."

"Oh, shame," said Jeremy. "My wife and I only just escaped the grind ourselves. But now we're looking to find a place where we can be a family. I've always dreamed of moving to a town like this."

"Do you have kids, then?"

"Just the one so far. A daughter, Melinda. Nine months."

Walter nodded. "That's a beautiful age. Any more on the way?"

"Not yet, but I'm working on it!"

"Well, best of luck to you on that. Anyway, I think you'll love it here. Come inside, I'll show you the view from the bedroom. It's the best in town!"

♦

As he showed Jeremy around, Walter eulogized the town. It had a multi-faith community with a strong church, a great school with a wonderful headmistress, and there were many other young families. Small farms on the outskirts provided almost all of the town's food—all fresh and locally grown.

He didn't mention the rest. It was impossible to get a Pepsi, for a start, or even a lousy fast-food hamburger. And that nine-month-old was going to *stay* nine months old for an awfully long time.

He wondered about that. Would they have been happier here if they'd moved here when Michael was a little older? Or when Jessica *hadn't* been suffering from morning sickness?

You couldn't leave—God knows they'd tried. You'd drive out of town along the same tree-lined road that you'd driven in on, but somewhere along the way you'd find yourself going back up the mountain instead of down it. You didn't turn around; you didn't have to. And somehow, you never saw it happen. They'd tried walking once, but it made no difference.

No mail got in from the outside, no television signals, no Wi-Fi. Every house had a phone, but you couldn't call out, and hardly any calls ever made it in. Nothing got out of Crescent Cross, and nothing from the outside was permitted in, save for those hoping to move in. And time seemed to be on the blacklist along with everything else.

Crescent Cross *had* time, but not like the rest of the world. You could move, throw balls, talk to the neighbors and chat about last week's drama, but nothing aged. There was precious little change at all. Even the weather was unchangeable, a relentless, balmy summer. It didn't stop people from celebrating Christmas, but it was strange decorating the tree in 90-degree weather.

The town itself changed very little too, and rarely. Nobody understood why or how. You'd wake up one day and there'd be anywhere from one to half a dozen new homes—bad news for anyone hoping to leave. The only way out was to sell your home.

Few wanted to. For most, Crescent Cross was Heaven on Earth. But *they* didn't have a two-year-old monster and a wife who had been sick all day, every single day, for the last 11 years.

Three times before, he'd tried to sell. Someone else had beaten him to it twice, and the third time the town had expanded and the buyers had moved into a brand-new home instead.

But this time, he was playing an entirely new game. He'd practiced by showing Jessica around the home, trying to sell it to her half a dozen times, tweaking the words, changing the focus. He left nothing to chance.

"And we're letting it go cheap," he said. "But only to someone we like, someone who really fits the town."

"Well, I sure hope you think I fit," said Jeremy.

"You sure do," said Walter. He smiled and clapped Jeremy on the back. "And if you decide to buy, then I've got a fine bottle of whiskey to share with you, 20 years old. Just say the word!"

The man was wavering. With the right word, Walter could sway him before he even went to look at the other homes. But the moment was lost.

"If I don't look at the others first, my wife will hang my guts out over the washing line," said Jeremy. "She's always telling me I jump into things without thinking it through."

"A smart lady," said Walter, as he swore inwardly. "But I'm telling you, you won't find a better deal. So I'll set the bottle aside, and I'll get some ice ready. You'll be back before the day's done, I guarantee it."

♦

As soon as Jeremy left, Walter hurried upstairs. His wife, who had put on a brave face while showing off the master bedroom, returned to the bathroom. How there was still anything left inside her to throw up was a mystery.

"Honey, he's off to see the Williams' cabin," said Walter. "Then he'll be heading on to the Metcalfe Lodge."

"Told you," she said. Her voice was weak, but determined. "Are you ready?"

"Sure am," he said. "It's time for part two."

♦

Jeremy liked the Williams' cabin, but it was too small. It might be a cozy spot for a retired couple, but it had too little room for a budding family. The McAllister house was nicer, and had a magnificent view, but the guy selling it had seemed a little weird. Something was off, and as much as he liked the home, he'd grown nervous about the idea of buying it.

Still, it was a nice place, and the guy wouldn't be there when they moved in, of course. But he still had high hopes for the Metcalfe Lodge.

Even from a distance, it was spectacular. A three-floor log cabin with a wall of windows, it had broad, low-fenced grounds with a great oak tree in the front and a marble-edged stone path leading to the front door.

"Hey, welcome," said a middle-aged man. He waved from his rocking chair and stood, his arms wide and a broad grin on his face. "I'm Lee Metcalfe. You're Jeremy?"

"Sure am."

"Then let me show you around! I promise you, this is the place you'll buy. It's the best home in the whole of Crescent Cross. It's got six bedrooms and four bathrooms, and a pool and a hot tub in the back." Lee led him along a path toward the back of the home. "Most of the houses here are a little old-fashioned. It makes for a lovely town, no doubt, but personally I like my creature comforts."

From behind the house, they heard a splash, and Lee frowned as he hurried around to the back. Jeremy followed him.

At first glance, the pool was a fine specimen of its kind—kidney-shaped, 100 feet long and 30 wide, with steps leading down into it. The stone that ringed the pool was white, but the scattered animal droppings on it detracted from the overall impression.

The raccoon swimming around the deep end didn't help it much, either.

"Well that's a first," said Lee. "They usually stay out near the farms."

"Don't they carry rabies?"

"What? Oh, not here, no! No, I don't think we've had a single case."

Jeremy frowned. The man was hardly going to jump up and say, "Yes, it's a rabies hotspot," now was he? But still, animals lived in the forest, and that meant droppings. Admittedly, a raccoon doing the breaststroke in the backyard was new, but that could be fixed. He could reinforce the fence easily enough. And it *was* a nice pool.

The raccoon hopped out and wandered off, leaving sodden footprints in its wake.

But that was only the beginning. When they got to the kitchen, a dark shape scurried out of sight, and a monstrous cockroach scuttled across the kitchen table. While the owner explained that "this isn't normal," a loud crunching noise came from the front of the house. The corner of the porch roof had collapsed, its wooden tiles were scattered all over the front lawn, and a fallen beam had crushed one of the rocking chairs.

"I'm not doing a good job of this," said Lee at last.

"That you aren't," said Jeremy. What if his wife had been sitting there when that had happened, or Melinda?

In the shadow of the oak tree, Walter saw Jeremy's expression and smiled. His work was done.

♦

But a week later, they still hadn't heard anything.

"You must've done it wrong," said Jessica miserably. "We're going to be stuck here! There's no way I'll survive another year of this!"

Not that she'd have a choice. Hank Sherman had escaped years earlier, but not before a string of suicide attempts. All he ever achieved was a lot of pain.

It was galling that they'd not heard back from the buyer, though. It had taken almost a fortnight to catch the raccoon, and finding a cockroach was tough; they were rare in Crescent Cross. The porch roof had been easier, and the buyer's face had convinced him that his work was done.

What had he missed? What *else* could he have done?

♦

Two days later, they had a visitor.

"Hey, Walt," said George, the Mayor of Crescent Cross. He looked around 50, though something about him simply reeked of age. "Well, it looks like you'll be leaving us."

"Oh, so he bought our place, did he? I knew he would! The view—"

"No, he bought the Metcalfe place in the end."

Walter frowned.

"So what's this about us leaving, then?"

"We got the papers this morning: an eviction notice and a demolition order."

"What?"

"Yeah, it's a first for me, too," said George, scratching his head. "McCullough said it's happened before, but I've never seen it. The best I can figure it, you did something that made the town upset. I guess you aren't welcome anymore."

Walter stood silently. They'd paid good money for the house, and selling it would have allowed them to buy a new one, a little place out in the Midwest maybe.

Still, out was out. And money or no, if he'd known he could escape just by pissing the town off, he'd have done it years ago.

"Well, easy come, easy go," he said with a grin.

♦

It didn't take them long to gather their things; most of their belongings were already boxed up in case the house had sold. The news that it hadn't sold didn't concern Jessica one bit. The only thing she cared about was getting out.

Within the hour, they had everything loaded into the car, and the two-year-old terror was strapped, screaming, into his car seat.

"Time to go," said Walter.

"And good riddance," said Jessica. She gave the house the finger.

They drove out to the tree-lined road and began descending. Soon they'd reach the point they'd never passed, and Walter felt his stomach knotting. What if they still turned around? Or what if the town just redirected them out over the edge of the mountain?

Well, what the Hell. Anything beat staying. He pushed down the gas pedal hard, and as they accelerated, a manic grin crept onto his face. They'd know soon, one way or the other.

"See you later, alligator," he sang.

They crossed the ridge at the edge of town, and the road began to whistle past them, fast—too fast, really, but he was beyond caring. He still expected to see Crescent Cross hover back into view, or the ground to vanish. But they kept going, and then he saw an unfamiliar sign approaching.

You are leaving Crescent Cross, it said. *Please come again!*

"We're out, baby!" he said. His wife was already laughing.

Crescent Cross

"We're out!"

In the back, Michael began laughing too, and Walter clapped the steering wheel.

"So, where shall we go?"

"Wherever's close," said his wife. "Oh, oh! Let's go to McDonald's! There's bound to be one close by! I haven't had a Big Mac in years!"

Walter grinned. Below the mountain was a regular town of 10,000 or so regular people, with regular food, regular weather, and if he remembered correctly, a regular McDonald's.

The trees remained thick, and there were only brief glimpses of the mountain's edge as they drove. Then ahead, he saw a sign approaching. It was dirty and rusted at the edges, but the text was clear.

Crescent Cross, population 141. Sister City of Belleville.

His wife fell silent. In the back, Michael was still laughing.

"Maybe we can't leave yet," he said. "Maybe we need to wait for the house to be demolished?"

But something was wrong. Crescent Cross was small, but not *that* small. The population had been nearly 2,000, and the sky above them was storm-gray, not summer blue. The air was cold, and snow kissed the roadside.

But it never snowed in Crescent Cross. Not even when you wanted it to.

As they crossed the ridge near the entrance to the town, he saw the town proper. A sprawling mass of old-mountain cabins, cottages, and small mansions stretched out almost as far as the eye could see; the lush forests of Crescent Cross had been cut back to make room. Almost all of them were in ruin. Some had already collapsed; the others were crumbling.

But at the side of the town, near the edge of the mountain, one home was brand-new.

Their home, still nestled in its prized spot, looking out toward that awful sunset view.

He parked up in the driveway and got out. The house was unchanged, save for the frost on the roof's tiles. Behind him, Jessica collected Michael from the car and went inside without a word.

He trudged around to help her move things inside, but as he lifted a box from the trunk, he saw an old man walking up the drive toward him, carrying a long, wrapped object. Walter set the box down, waved, and walked over with a smile.

"Hey, neighbor," he called. "The name's—"

The wrapping fell away, and the old man thrust a makeshift spear up toward his neck. It was just a knife tied to a stick, but it would be more than enough to kill him.

"Food," he said. His voice was low, cracked with age, and one of the eyes that stared out of his head was cloudy with cataracts. "And any guns you have."

Walter raised his hands. "Look, man, I've got a wife. And a kid."

"So think fast. Quickly, now, or I swear I'll—"

There was a sudden howl from the sky. Walter looked up. The clouds began painting across the sky in broad streaks, and the sun and moon flew past like glowing rockets. Shadows grew long and short in seconds, and in front of him, the old man groaned and dropped the spear.

Wispy, white hair grew long from the old man's head and chin as his good eye clouded over, and with a choking gasp, he fell to the ground.

The sky quieted. Walter bent down, grabbed the spear, and checked the old man. There was no pulse, and …

He reached up to his own face. A beard was there now, at least two inches, maybe longer. A long wisp of bangs brushed over his eyes.

Inside, he could hear Michael screaming.

"Walter!" His wife's voice was half cry, half howl.

"Walter, it's coming now!"

He ran inside, still clutching the spear tight. Michael was crying in the corner, his tormented shrieks filling the room, and Jessica was on the floor in a puddle of liquid.

The baby!

Were there Doctors? Hospitals? No, he'd seen the whole town, and their chances were slim to none. How would he trust a doctor even if he found one? They were on their own. And as he looked at his wife, his mind ran back to the hurried sky.

They were on their own, but for how long?

Please come again!

For the first time in years, he wished he could.

Kentucky Rush
by Samuel Marzioli

Megan entered the grocery store looking every bit the part of a vagrant, tramping through to escape the broiling summer heat. The thought even occurred to her when she passed the glass doors of the frozen foods aisle and sneaked a glance at her reflection. There wasn't much she could do about it now, so she swept a hand through the tangles of her hair, to break apart the stiffness, and shrugged and carried on.

She pulled a mangled slip of notebook paper from her purse and read her grocery list from top to bottom. Most of the items had been written down at home during a rare energetic fit, but that feeling had quickly passed and she mentally crossed out the majority of them on the drive over. Only sandwich ingredients remained, and that suited her just fine. Sandwiches were easy: just a few slices of bread, a slather of something sweet or tart, and the meal was finished.

After gathering peanut butter, jelly, mayonnaise, mustard, and some lunchmeat, Megan rolled her cart to the last stop: the bread aisle. That was when she saw something framed between the endcap's empty shelves. From a distance, it looked almost like a face peering at her from around the corner, utterly black but for the whites of its eyes. She squinted, trying to extract detail, but she couldn't quite pull meaning from the anomalous blur.

"Hello?" she said, taking a step forward.

From the size of it, she thought it might be a child no older than ten or twelve. But were they merely playing a game with her, or lost and scared and waiting for a parent?

"Tommy?" she said, though she didn't know why.

She drew within 20 feet of the aisle's end before the shape moved at last, confirming at least some of her suspicions. She was wrong about one thing, though: it wasn't a child or anything remotely human. It shifted away from her advance, not so much turning as folding on itself, the soft, doughy substance of its body twisting and pulling until it faced the other way. Once it stood in the light of the back aisle, its dark form lessened by a degree, revealing a subtle transparency, as if it were a shadow that had peeled itself from the ground and began to walk upright.

It sidled to its left and slipped out of sight. She hurried after it, her curiosity proving stronger than her bewilderment. With each step, the aisle lengthened before her, forming walls along the borders of her vision. Nervous energy bloomed within her, exploding into wild panic as she felt herself pulled forward and yanked into the air. Once she hovered level with the fluorescent lighting, she screamed, flailing her limbs, struggling to free herself from the mysterious force that held her aloft.

"Help me!" she cried. "Please, someone help me!" and then--

She found herself on the floor again. Standing by the bread shelves. Still gripping her cart.

A few sideways glances revealed that no one had witnessed her hallucination, or mental breakdown, or whatever it had been. With a heavy sigh, she rolled her cart to the checkout stand, humming a tune to mask the frantic beating of her heart.

♦

Megan awoke early the next day and toddled to the living room. She didn't bother calling in sick for work. In fact, she hadn't bothered calling in sick for a while now. Her boss, Mr. White, had been accommodating for the most part.

"I'm sorry. What you've been through is just terrible," he'd said. "If you need some time off, I fully understand."

But that understanding hadn't stretched much farther than a month, and now she was pushing up against two. She seemed to recall hearing an apologetic ultimatum at some point in the interim: if she didn't return to work, she was finished with the company. Maybe there had even been a phone call from Mr. White confirming her firing as recently as two weeks ago. She couldn't remember and couldn't quite bring herself to care.

For the rest of the morning, she watched TV, balling up slices of bread because the time required by making a sandwich was too much of a bother. After five episodes of soap operas, talk shows, and one news program, she spotted the shadow-thing again, this time streaking by the glass of her patio door. She hurried to an open window and peered outside.

"Hello?" she shouted. "I know you're there!"

She didn't expect an answer. She only meant to convince whomever, or whatever, it was that she wasn't afraid.

The longer she searched the wide expanse of her backyard, the more a series of smells wafted to her nose: meat sizzling on an open grill, fried dough, the sweet scent of cotton candy. Her vision darkened and her thoughts drifted back to the amusement park where she'd almost lost her life.

The memory of months past was just as hazy as the present, but she could easily picture that windy Santa Clara day--details so stark it raised gooseflesh across her arms and legs--and she breathed in deep the bay's salty, briny scent. She remembered standing inside the fragmented shadow of the roller coaster, staring up at the bones of its frame, listening to all the helpless riders screaming.

"Don't let it scare you," Uncle Frank had said, noticing her hesitation. "The Kentucky Rush is harmless."

He ruffled her hair, which was strange because he never ruffled her hair, not since she was a child. It must have worked its reassuring magic because, in that moment, she actually believed him. But experience soon taught her that her trust had been misplaced. The danger had been real.

A tickle on her lip broke her concentration. She lifted a hand to wipe the tears away, but froze when she caught a better glimpse of the shadow-thing at last. It stood beside the fence, darting to the outer edge of clarity before she could see it plain: some unknown quadruped that dropped on ample haunches, slavering through a crop of tangled teeth, its eyes full and wide and staring.

♦

Seven visits in seven days from the shadow-thing had taken a serious toll on Megan. No matter how hard she tried, she couldn't sleep and she longed for the comfort of empty dreams to save her from her waking life.

Still dressed in pajamas, she sat on her bed, scanning the framed photos on the dresser. For some reason, she found it far more difficult to recall those days, those memories, than anything else from the past. The only thing she knew for sure was that they represented important moments in her life.

One showed a vacant playground with a swing caught mid-sway by some strong breeze. One showed her and Uncle Frank standing apart, their arms held toward each other, but not touching. The last was a shot of her boyfriend Gabriel at the wharf, measuring the ocean air with the flat of his hand. The sight of them made her sad, churning her stomach until she nearly vomited. In fact, crying had become a regular occurrence ever since that shadow-thing had appeared. And always, thoughts of the amusement park bled into her mind.

She felt certain that the incident on the Kentucky Rush had brought that creature to life, though she couldn't piece together how or why. She remembered standing in line with Uncle Frank and Gabriel, how they had insisted she ride despite her protestations and the many hot tears sliding down her cheeks.

Once she was locked into her seat, the train had raced through a lightless tunnel and ascended the lift hill. She sucked in air. Then came the drop that knocked her breathless, even as the safety bar came loose and snatched away a scream. Each twist and turn thereafter crumbled hidden walls inside her mind, until nothing remained but the permeating black behind her eyelids, stretching longer than the infinite loop of tracks.

When the coaster came to a halt, she scrambled for the platform, scratching at the seams of its tightly knit planks until her fingernails tore and bled. She looked around. The world opened up to her. Only it was tainted, a touch of blur swallowing the details, everything cast in a darker shade.

That was when she saw it, black as coal, moving too fast to follow in her disoriented state. She lost track of it once security came and brought her to the manager's office. Hours passed before the police allowed her to leave. By then, it was nowhere to be seen and she promptly forgot about it.

Now she couldn't think of anything else.

♦

Megan remained shut in, afraid to leave her room. The shadow-thing continued prowling the perimeter of her house, rattling the bolted front door, pulling or pushing on each sealed window as if searching for a way in. And then on the tenth day, on its tenth visit, it found one.

It was in the early morning. While rushing through the hallway on her way to the toilet, Megan glanced through the doorway of the spare bedroom. There, among the clutter of taped boxes, filled plastic bags, and scattered toys, a crack appeared in the opposite wall, thin as a line drawn by felt marker, but deep enough to touch the outside air.

Her heart drubbed against her ribs and her muscles clenched. Somehow, she knew that crack would be wide enough to let the shadow-thing in. She wracked her brain, trying to think up quick fixes within her means: duct tape, crazy glue, a blanket and staples. Instead, she slammed the door and held it shut, knowing all too well that two inches of hollow wood was only a slightly better option.

Within seconds, a slowly mounting creak arose. A sudden, violent crack almost made her turn and run, but she held on tight, tugging at the knob, strengthened by an unshakable will to live. Footsteps trailed closer, not the click of nails upon the floorboards that she expected, but the soft patter of feet, one step after the other. It drew up, thrust its weight into the door and its center bowed and crackled.

Megan gritted her teeth, bracing herself. Memories of the roller coaster emerged again. A high-pitched scream echoed in her ears, filling the emptiness of her insides with the same loss and isolation that had claimed her on the Kentucky Rush. But this time, it didn't have the same disconnected quality of her other trance-like memories. This time it came from a source mere inches from her face.

The knob twisted. She fell back and began scampering crablike away from the opening door. Once she found the entryway, she scrambled to her feet and fled the house, stopping only to jump into her car before putting miles of road between her and home.

♦

Megan called Gabriel and made plans for lunch at Westfield Center, a five-story mall that was among the busiest sites in San Francisco. After all that isolation, she wanted mobs, needed noise. But more than anything, she believed it would be a place the shadow-thing would never dare to follow. A small-town grocery store and a suburban house were one thing, but a bustling metropolis was quite another.

She remembered driving and a sliver of her and Gabriel's conversation, but little else in between until she spotted him traipsing down Market Street in her direction. He threw his arms around her before she had a chance to pull away. For a moment, she could smell herself: the sick, ripe scent of body odor. It made her gag, so she disengaged from their embrace quicker than he'd wanted.

"I didn't know if I'd ever hear from you again," he said into her ear.

"Let's hurry," she said, taking his hand and pulling him toward the crosswalk.

Though the streets seemed safer than her home, it still felt too exposed. Somewhere, drifting below the surface of her mind, she knew she was afraid. She also knew she could push that feeling deeper into her subconscious until it vanished beyond perception. In fact, she'd gotten quite good at it and did so now to calm her mounting trembles.

"I've been meaning to call," said Gabriel.

"It's been a long week. I might not have answered."

"I can't even begin to imagine." He stopped and examined her, taking in every inch.

"What?" said Megan, turning to face him, her cheeks reddening.

"Nothing. It's just …" He shook his head and smiled. "There's no good way to put this. You look terrible. I feel partially to blame; I know you told me you needed time and space to process everything that's happened, but I should have been there for you. It's not healthy for you to be by yourself, that much is obvious. From now on, I'm not leaving your side until you learn to put all this behind you."

Megan's fingers collapsed into a fist around his hand. She wanted to shout, "It's only been two months, God damn it," and jump on him, and scratch, and tear and bite at every inch of that sympathetic expression. But something big coursed through the throng of people behind them, shoving them away as if they were as trivial as limp rag dolls. Before she could gather her wits, the shadow-thing broke out into the open and lunged at her.

"Watch out!" she screamed.

She knocked Gabriel aside and dived away, crashing headlong onto the pavement. She managed to prop herself up fast enough to see the backside of the creature, racing in the distance, a splotch of black that disappeared into the streaming masses.

It took some time before she noticed Gabriel, lying in the street, his head crushed by the wheel of a trolleybus.

♦

In the panic that erupted from the gathering crowd, Megan slipped away unnoticed. How she got back to her car and on the road again, she didn't have a clue. But she did know where she would head next. With Gabriel gone, Uncle Frank was the only one who could help her now.

She pulled into Uncle Frank's driveway beside his Buick, the same vehicle they had used to carpool to that amusement park. A quick glimpse of that day flooded her mind, with Uncle Frank behind the wheel, an inelegant chauffeur caterwauling some country tune, and in the back seat, her and Gabriel and... But the pain of Gabriel's death yanked the thought away, and she stumbled from her car to the front porch.

Uncle Frank didn't seem surprised when he opened up the door and found her standing on the doorstep, weeping. He just swept his arm out in welcome. She followed him to the living room where he dropped into his recliner, guzzling a bottle of whiskey and glancing sidelong between her and the wall.

She spent the next few minutes taking deep, stuttered breaths, to bring about some measure of calm.

"He's dead," she said at last.

Uncle Frank sighed. "Do you think I don't know that?"

"But--"

"Look, Megan, if I were a stronger man, maybe I could let you talk about it for as long as you needed. But I'm not. Not today. Maybe not ever."

She shook her head. Confusion rattled in her skull. Had she already told him about Gabriel on the phone? She didn't remember making any calls, not that remembering meant anything anymore, since that skill had lapsed after her accident. She was about to ask what he'd meant, but she heard the shadow-thing's scream and her throat locked around the words. Distorted by the distance, it sounded like a goat with its throat slit, pouring garbled bleats through the bleeding gash.

"Oh, God. It's here," she said, casting anxious looks around.

Uncle Frank rose from his chair, set the bottle down slowly. "What? What is it?" he said.

The scream came again, now much closer, spewing from the mouth of something just outside the house. She turned to Uncle Frank and they held each other's gaze. Her bottom lip quivered.

"Hide," she said.

Before either of them could move, the shadow-thing leapt through the curtains of an open window and pounced on Uncle Frank. Megan ran to the kitchen and grabbed a knife. She returned to find Uncle Frank on the floor, his shrieks smothered beneath the creature's massive form, its razor-sharp claws ravaging his body.

She rushed at it, swinging her weapon with manic fervor, slicing down its flank and across its bulging eyes. One deep thrust into its cheek and it slinked away, back through the window and into the dark of night.

Once she regained her composure, she turned to Uncle Frank. Her jaw went slack when she saw his vacant eyes, the wounds covering his body, the many cuts extending deep into his chest and face. She'd been too slow to save him. And now she was alone.

♦

Stuffed inside the thick foliage of a bush, Megan waited for the amusement park to close. Hours passed before the din of summer customers faded and silence finally settled over the lot. Carrying a metal pipe she'd found beneath a plastic tarp by the southern fence, she crawled from her hiding place and made her way across the asphalt to the Kentucky Rush.

As expected, she spotted the shadow-thing prowling a distant stretch of tracks--its birthplace and its home. While she knew confronting it was tantamount to suicide, she also knew she didn't have any other choice. It had already taken Gabriel and Uncle Frank, and as long as it lived, she would never know peace again.

With a running start, she hopped the ride's entrance gate, crossed the platform and began her ascent. Though the wooden cross-ties were closely spaced, she gripped each one like the tenuous holds of a cliff face, always looking up, never at the increasing drop between each rung.

The shadow-thing met her at the tallest peak, its white sclera deepening the blackness of its body. It didn't charge as she expected; it simply slumped down against the tracks, waiting. Megan didn't care why; the opportunity was all that mattered. She took a step up, raised the pipe, and swung. Her first blow caught the thing across its temple. Another found its mouth, shattering a row of teeth. One more against its front leg and it fell from its perch, plummeting down to the concrete foundation far below her.

Drained of energy, she collapsed to the cross-ties, unable to move. A sudden throbbing ache in her head made it difficult to think. She tasted blood. After taking a few sharp, shallow breaths, she tried to climb back down. The second her foot touched the next step, her leg, and then her entire body, exploded in agony. The world shifted piece by piece, assembling in a different order--

And she found herself smashed into the ground beside the hulking roller coaster.

In that moment, she remembered everything. Tommy was her son. He'd been in every photo on her dresser: on the swing, between her and Uncle Frank, beneath Gabriel's hand at the wharf. The spare room had even been his bedroom before she'd stuffed his things in bags and boxes and pushed it out of sight.

What's more, Tommy had been there with them in the roller coaster line. As they passed between the partition ropes, they chose to ignore his pleas, his tears, the abject fear in his expression. They had even laughed when he said the safety bar didn't click, thinking he was just being chicken. But the bar snapped up at the first drop and he screamed as he was ripped from his seat beside her.

The shock of it had destroyed her. From then on, she refused to acknowledge Tommy, choosing to bury all thought of him to alleviate the torment of burying his body. Her mind was a mirror reflecting lies, but somewhere inside she'd always known the truth: that she, Uncle Frank, and Gabriel had been to blame for her son's death.

Tommy crept up beside her, no longer a monster, now a little boy again. As he stared down at her, he glowed in the soft blue shade of moonlight pouring through his body.

"You ... tricked me. You made me kill them," she said, gagging on the blood pooling in her mouth. "And you made me kill me, too."

Tommy fixed her with a cold, hard glare and nodded. His lips stretched into something like a smile, but there was no mirth in it.

Megan struggled to reach for him, but couldn't move. She almost formed the words, "Oh baby. I'm so, so sorry," but she knew it would be worthless. His face, all that hurt and pain and rage behind his eyes, said everything she needed to know. He'd never forgive her. He'd never forgive any of them.

Soon, her thoughts slipped away and her vision blurred. She closed her eyes, but she didn't find the peace of all-encompassing darkness that she'd expected. Instead, there was only the Kentucky Rush. It took hold of her and dragged her along the endless length of its tracks, stretching beyond the limits of her sight and into the black void of the horizon.

Road Kill

by R. Y. Brockway

I'd been working with Leon for a week when I noticed he had a knack for identifying roadkill.

"'Possum," he'd call 500 feet before we passed the carcass, or "'coon." When business took us south, the occasional "'dillo" entered the mix. No matter what it was, he never missed.

I played along for a time, learning how to identify the tell-tale markings of matted fur. But after six months of spider-webbing our way across the map, my taste for the game and Leon's company began to wane.

Leon's peculiarities weren't limited to just roadkill. He was anal about always having to drive—which was fine by me, because he chattered nonstop whenever his hands weren't busy, complaining endlessly about the engineered decking company that employed us or the shoppers who frequented the big-box hardware stores where we set up displays. His grousing wasn't limited to the car, either.

On more than one occasion, he'd stop working to lean over and whisper to me, "Hey, Ryan, you see that guy?"

I'd turn to find a man reading a can of weed killer, or a woman navigating a cart through the obstacle strewn aisles.

"Punk thinks he's better than us."

It was dumbfounding; those customers barely even registered our existence. But when I'd point that out to Leon, he would only sneer and remind me of the years he held over me both in life and on the road. He knew, he'd say, and in time, so would I.

This irked me to no end, but there was nothing I could do about it.

Back home, my wife and newborn son depended on my paycheck. Asking for a new partner was akin to turning in your resignation. So my days became a series of resigned shrugs, and I made sure to keep a novel on hand each time we got in the car so I could bury my nose in its pages while Leon drove.

If he noticed my sudden silence, or how I averted my eyes when he pointed out another victim of the freeway, he never acknowledged it, except to complain about the mountain of paperbacks piling up in the backseat.

I was on a true-crime kick when summer came and business took us through the backcountry of the Carolinas. We'd just finished a job in Greenville, where I'd picked up a new novel to tide me over until we reached Atlanta. I cracked the spine the moment we turned south.

The car's radio slid between frequencies on scan as we drove, occasionally landing on the notes of a twangy guitar or a preacher expounding on the gospel. For once, there was near-silence in the car, and I settled back into my seat, losing myself in the underbelly of Skid Row for 40 pages before a strange utterance from the driver's seat drew me back out.

"Now, what in the hell is that?"

I glanced up and spotted the crumpled mass on the side of the road.

"Jesus, Leon, it's probably been sitting in that ditch for days. Just keep going."

But we were already slowing down, the car listing to one side as its tires sank into the soft soil of the cotton field.

Leon cut the engine. "I'm going to check it out. You want to come with me?"

I shook my head no. He pulled the keys from the ignition. I groaned in protest, but he ignored me. Shaking my head, I rolled down my window and watched as he picked his way along the wayside toward the dark clump in the overgrown grass.

"Jesus," I repeated.

Road Kill

I tried to settle back into my book, but the muggy air rising off the cotton field permeated the car and I found myself rereading the same paragraph over and over. After the umpteenth time, I gave up and unbuckled my seatbelt.

A breeze from the east brought some relief from the humidity as I stepped out of the car. Stretching, I watched Leon poke around in the ditch. He scratched his head as he peered downward. This really was too much; we were due at our next appointment in just a few hours.

I cupped my hands to my mouth and shouted, "Leon! Come on, man, we've got places to be!"

He turned, but only for a moment. "Get the tire iron!" he called back, taking another step down into the ditch.

Frowning, I swatted at an insect circling my head. The only way I could see to get Leon back in the car was if I assisted him in his morbid fascination. Reluctantly, I fetched the tire iron from the trunk.

There was a cloud of flies undulating over the crumpled remains. Their droning was audible. I covered my mouth but still gagged when I knelt over the ditch to hand Leon the tire iron.

"Jesus, what is that?"

Leon shot me an "I told you so" glare.

A giant wing the length of a man's arm stuck out at an odd angle from what you might call the body of the thing. Its greasy black feathers bristled in the breeze and for a moment, I thought it might be a large turkey vulture. But that didn't explain the matted black fur covering the rest of the carcass.

Leon hefted the tire iron in his hand. "Thing ain't got a face. Maybe if I turn it over?"

"Leon, I don't think—" I stopped when he slid the pry end of the tire iron under the largest section of the animal. Viscous strands of semi-translucent mucus seeped from the mass as he lifted it from the ground.

"Kneel down, tell me if you can see anything," he grunted.

"Leon, no—"

He fixed me with a measuring stare. "Don't you want to know what it is?"

I looked back at the carcass. The disturbed flies dispersed, their buzzing now a distant hum. I swallowed and climbed down into the ditch. Leon was right; I did want to know. All those crime books had got me going. I couldn't ignore this mystery.

I got down on all fours. The downy heads of the seeding grass found their way up my shorts and tickled my skin as I pressed my face to the ground.

"I can't see anything," I called. "It's too dark." I was about to say it was too dead when a familiar shape caught my eye—it appeared to be a small shoe. I inched closer, stretching out my arm. My fingers brushed against the sticky strings of ooze as I reached for the sneaker.

Coughing and gripping my prize by the laces, I crawled back out of the ditch. The shoe was coated with slime, but beneath it, I saw the little white star printed on the ankle of the canvas high-top. A chill ran down my spine. I had a pair just like it when I was a boy.

"What is it?"

In my distraction, I'd forgotten about Leon. I held up the shoe for him to see. It twisted in the air, dangling from its laces. He took a long, hard look at it, his expression twisting into an unpleasant scowl when he recognized what it was.

"Son of a bitch!" Leon let the carcass drop. "It's a costume or mannequin or something. Someone's idea of a joke."

His anger took me off-guard. I thought he'd be proud at the lengths I'd gone to satisfy his curiosity. When a fly descended and landed on his neck, Leon smacked it in his fury. A white handprint blossomed on the red flush creeping up his neckline.

He roared, turning on me. The tire iron whistled past my face, just missing my upraised arm. It landed with a thwack against the canvas sneaker, and the laces tore from my fingers. The shoe went sailing end-over-end into the cotton field.

"What the fuck!" I rounded on Leon, preparing to strike back. His face was pale now, his eyes turned inward. I'd never seen him like that before, and it was enough to make me hesitate. "Leon, I don't think it's a joke, just a coincidence. I mean, there's always debris along the road, thrown out a window or fallen from an overloaded cargo carrier."

He glared at me and I pressed my lips tight, averting my eyes to look back over the cotton field. I could see the broken branches where the sneaker had landed, and in that moment, my stomach dropped. It was an odd thing to find, I had to admit. Leon's paranoia only added to my own misgivings and memories of insidious goings-on from those detective novels. The shoe had been small, so very small, and how had it ended up under that thing?

A siren and the crackling of tires slowing on the edge of the road broke my contemplation.

"Crap." I turned just in time to see a cop car roll up beside us.

"You having some trouble, boys?" A state trooper leaned out the window, his mirrored sunglasses catching our reflection, small and distant, in a double image on either side of his nose. "Need me to call you a tow?"

"No, officer," Leon said. "Just stretching our legs before we get back on our way."

The trooper peered over his glasses with professional suspicion.

"On your way? Not unless you've got two spares instead of the usual one."

Leon's head snapped around and I followed his gaze to our car. He cursed loudly as I gaped at the set of deflated tires on the passenger's side.

We waited as the trooper radioed in the incident. When it was reported back it would be some time before a tow could come, he offered us a ride into town. Leon protested, but in the end, we climbed into the back of the squad car.

The trooper apologized through the wire screen separating us from the driver's seat.

"Sorry, but in these parts, nothing happens fast. Not much of anything that needs hurrying. I'll drop you at the Silver Spoon, you can wait there until Barry gets around to fixing you up."

Leon snorted. I tried to make up for his callousness by thanking the trooper for not leaving us to bake in the sun while we waited for "Barry's" dubious arrival. I'm not sure Leon agreed. He fidgeted next to me the whole ride, barely speaking a word.

The trooper let us out on a corner. I watched him make a U-turn and head back toward the highway, then I checked my watch. It was just past two. There was no telling when we would be getting back on the road.

"Why don't you go inside and get us a booth?" I said to Leon, nodding in the direction of a neon sign shaped like a giant soup spoon. "I'll call the boss and let him know we're gonna be late."

It was obvious that Leon wasn't thrilled with the idea. It meant I was taking control. But at the moment, he wasn't looking too good. His hair was askew, his eyes bloodshot, and there was a red lump rising from where he'd slapped at his neck earlier. He scratched at it with annoyance.

"Yeah, you do that. Too damn hot out here anyways."

I waited for the diner's door to close behind him before fishing out my cell phone.

I perused my surroundings as I waited for our boss to answer. The state trooper was right; the town wasn't much—a short row of two-story brick buildings along a main drag with what I assumed was Barry's garage at the far end. It was quaint and a bit rundown, but nostalgic in a Mayberry kind of way. The type of place, I was certain, where everyone knew each other.

"Hello?" A gruff voice broke the staticky barrage of rings in my ear.

Shouting over the bad signal, I explained our predicament to the boss. Leon was right about one thing: the home office had no respect for us guys on the road. I found myself agreeing to drive all night to our next stop if that would make things right, just to stop the flow of grievances from the other end of the line.

My boss put me on hold while he looked for the number of a night manager. Patting my pockets for something to write on, I found nothing, so I tore down an old flier that had fallen loose from the light pole closest to me. When our boss came back on the line, I scribbled the digits he rattled off on the back of the rain-stained paper.

Snapping shut my phone, I felt a twinge of Leon's deep-seated annoyance. It wasn't fair. I hadn't done anything wrong. The overwhelming sensation that I deserved better than this, that my life was going nowhere, mingled with the dread of the grousing I would have to endure when I delivered the bad news to Leon.

I leaned my head back and sighed.

All I wanted was to go home, to lie in my own bed for one night and be comforted by my wife and her unrelenting sympathy. *If I could just hear her voice*, I thought, *I might be okay.* But when I looked back down at my phone, I saw the reception had gone from a single faint bar to a null void of service.

In frustration, I lashed out at the wall next to me and came away with scraped and bloody knuckles. I sucked at the wound as I made my way to the diner.

"They're still serving breakfast," Leon slid me a laminated menu when I took the seat across from him. "What'd you do to your hand?"

"Accident," I mumbled, feigning interest in the specials. "Boss wants us to drive all night to make up the time."

Soft chuckling came from across the table instead of the rage and cursing I was expecting.

"What's so funny?"

Leon picked up the pepper and unscrewed the lid, then screwed it on tighter before shaking it over his eggs. "What'd you expect, Ryan, you think the old bastard would give us a break?"

"No. I—"

Leon exchanged the shaker for his fork. "You know what your problem is, Ryan? You want to deny what's right in front of you." He pointed at my bloody knuckles. "You'd be much happier if you just accepted the world for what it is and stopped making excuses for people you barely know."

I crossed my arms over my chest. "Oh, I suppose I'd be better off taking a page from your book and assuming everyone's out to get me?"

Leon shrugged. "At least I don't get upset when people act the way I expect them to."

I balked at his hypocrisy. "You're telling me—the guy whose head you almost took off with a tire iron—that you don't get upset? That's good, Leon, that's real good."

He chewed for a moment. "That was different. I was sticking up for us. I don't like to look like a fool."

The last of my patience broke and I snorted. "A fool? That's what you're worried about? Well you're no fool, Leon. You're a loser; that's what you are. You got no friends, no family. You could disappear and no one would notice." I pointed at my chest. "All you've got is a captive audience to listen to your rails against the world, and half the time, I'm not even listening. You know why? Because it's all bullshit."

Leon's cheeks flushed. I'd gone too far and I knew it.

"Look, I'm sorry," I said. "I'm hot, I'm tired, and we've got a long drive ahead of us. Let's just eat in peace, okay?"

But Leon was having none of that. He stood, pulled his wallet from his back pocket, and yanked out two twenties.

"You go on pretending we're so different." He stared down at me, his voice a hoarse whisper. "But we got the same job; we wear the same shirts on our backs. Yeah, maybe I ain't got no family, but I bet that boy of yours you're always going on about doesn't even recognize his own daddy. When's the last time you saw him, Ryan? Huh? When you can remember that, then we'll talk about who's a loser and who's not."

He threw down the money and stormed out.

I sat there seething, my mouth twisting as I chewed the words he'd flung at me. Leon would never understand my sacrifice, what I was going through to give my family a leg up. And my son, he was still just a baby. But my blood chilled as I realized it'd been a dozen or more weeks since I'd been home. My boy, who had only been six months old when I accepted this job, would be saying his first words any day now. I thought back to that shoe, and how things can fall by the wayside when you aren't looking.

"Your friend coming back?"

I looked up and saw a young waitress standing at my table. I looked with dismay at Leon's barely touched plate of food.

"I don't know."

"Well, you want to order, or you want to wait?" The waitress popped her gum.

"Just give me whatever he was having." I'd lost my appetite.

I picked at my food for an hour, certain Leon would come back after he blew off steam. But an hour stretched into two and there was still no sign of him. I regretted leaving my novel back in the car, desperate for something to distract me from the words that had been said. I made do with a copy of the local paper, half-skimming the articles as I glanced at the door and checked my phone to see if to see if I had a message, only to be disappointed.

After three hours, the dinner crowd began to trickle in. I could no longer ignore the fact that Leon probably wouldn't return on his own, that I'd have to go find him. Hopefully that would be enough to patch things up, and he wouldn't make me admit he'd been right.

I paid the check and left the waitress Leon's two twenties for her patience.

My shadow fell long and lean across the cracked sidewalk when I stepped outside. I shielded my eyes from the low-hanging sun and searched the street for Leon. It was empty, as it had been earlier, but parked outside Barry's garage, there was a rusted old tow truck. Figuring Leon had seen the same thing, I hurried in that direction.

I was pretty irritated by the time I reached the open bays of the garage, expecting to find Leon chatting up the mechanic with no consideration for the fact that I'd been waiting. But when I ducked inside, there was no sign of Leon, just our bug-splattered sedan up on a lift and a bearded man in coveralls rolling a tire over from a rack in the back.

"This your car, fella?"

"You must be Barry." He nodded and I offered my hand as he stood. "Yeah it's my—our car. I was hoping my partner would be here already." I craned my neck to look around.

Barry mopped his brow with a rag. "Haven't seen anybody since I got in a few minutes ago. Sorry to keep y'all waiting. But you're lucky, I've got your size in stock, won't take but a jiffy for me to get you back up and running."

His friendly smile didn't put me much at ease. I pulled out my cell phone to check the time and to see if my service had miraculously returned.

"You got a phone I could try to call him on?"

Barry hooked a thumb over his shoulder. "You can use the office line if you don't stay on too long."

I thanked him and found my way inside.

Surprisingly, Leon's cell rang when I dialed, but after a few short hums, it rolled over to voicemail. I hung up and tried again, receiving the same abrupt message to leave my name and number. I left a voicemail this time: the car is ready, meet me at the garage, we need to put this day behind us.

After I hung up, I felt that maybe I should have apologized more. But what was Leon playing at, making me wait around like this? He already gotten his pound of flesh, that shot he took about the kind of father I was turning into. But this was way beyond his normal shenanigans, and I couldn't help but feel a little worried. It was getting dark now. What could he be getting up to in a town this small?

I fished out the night manager's number, figuring I should let him know we still hadn't left. The call was answered by a robotic voice which insisted on listing the store's hours and weekly specials before getting to the departmental extensions. I tapped the edge of the scrap of paper on the desk as I waited. Then, out of sheer boredom, I turned it over to glance at the back. When I saw what was printed there, I hung up the phone.

"You get ahold of your friend?"

Startled, I looked up. Barry was standing in the doorway.

"No. I mean—look." I wiped my lips. "I didn't realize what I was doing, but I think I destroyed an important poster."

I looked back down at the half-torn piece of paper and grimaced. The picture was grainy, but you could still make out the boy's mischievous grin, the word "missing," and a name that was still legible despite the water stains: Elliott Daniels.

I handed it to Barry and his eyebrows rose.

"Oh, this. I thought we'd taken all of these down." He shook his head. "You don't need to worry about this."

"Why not? Did they find him?" *God, please let him say yes.*

"Oh, they found him alright. Hiding out in a fort him and his friends built back in the woods. Had a fight with his mom and thought he'd give her a little scare. We've been having a rash of adolescent mischief lately. Sorry you had to fall victim to it a second time."

I must have looked dumbfounded, because he handed back the slip of paper rather sheepishly.

"Look, I'm not going to charge you for my labor, just the tires. I'd hate for a stranger to get the wrong impression about our town. I'll make sure the hoodlums who slashed your tires are dealt with."

I swallowed, my stomach turning sour as what he said sank in. Slashed tires? Had Leon been right? Had today's events all stemmed from some kid's idea of a practical joke?

My head was still reeling when I settled the bill. I didn't think twice when Barry handed me the keys. It wasn't until I was out in the parking lot, about to unlock the car, that I realized something was wrong. Leon had pulled the keys from the ignition when we stopped on the highway. How had Barry gotten ahold of them?

I turned on my heel, determined to get to the bottom of this, but I found that the windows of the garage had gone dark. There was no sign of Barry or his tow truck.

I tried to convince myself that there was some reasonable explanation. Maybe Barry had slipped out a back door. Maybe someone else came to get the truck. But when I opened the car door and sat down in the driver's seat, I couldn't help but think that maybe Leon had also been right when he told me in the diner that I needed to stop making excuses for people I barely knew. There was something about this town, this day, that didn't sit right. The sooner it was all behind me, the better.

But I couldn't leave without Leon.

I slid the driver's seat forward and started the engine. The iron lampposts flicked on as I turned out on to the main street, their garish light making the shadows of the darkened storefronts even more ominous. I checked each one as I passed. No Leon. Only the Silver Spoon appeared to be inhabited. Through the plate-glass window, I could see the same waitress who'd served me lunch, leaning against the counter. She was absentmindedly twirling something in her hand as she stared off into space. It took me a second before I recognized it as a flyswatter.

I turned off the main road and began searching the side streets.

Twilight sank into true night, and still I couldn't find him. I was about to turn back on to the main street, head back to the diner, and ask if I could use their phone, when my pocket vibrated and trilled. I slammed on the breaks, afraid that if I moved another inch I'd lose the signal.

"Ryan?" Leon's voice crackled over the earpiece and for once, I was happy to hear it.

"Leon, where are you? Do you have any idea what time it is?"

"Ryan—" A hiss of static broke the connection.

I realized he couldn't hear me so I listened for some clue to his whereabouts.

"Ryan, are you there? I need you to come get me."

I wasn't sure, but there seemed to be some sound in the background. No, not in the background, there was something different about Leon's voice. Was he sobbing?

"Leon!" I shouted. "Leon!"

There was heavy breathing on Leon's end. "Please, you have to— I'm on the high—by that—Please, oh God—"

The line went dead.

I laid on the gas, ignoring the posted speed limit. The new tires squealed as I turned back onto the main street and tore up the road in the direction of the highway. Dark fields whizzed by in my peripheral vision, as questions about how and why Leon had made it back to the highway raced through my head.

There was no traffic when I turned off the bypass. I slowed to the safest crawl I thought possible, searching in the narrow beam of the headlights for someone stranded on the shoulder. But the shadows of night loomed in all around me, rising like mist from the surrounding fields, making it impossible to see anything but the dotted yellow line of the road ahead.

Twenty minutes later, I reached the next turnoff. I pulled over and stared at the sign for a moment as I contemplated how I was going to find Leon in these conditions. I glanced at the dashboard, and the amber glow of the clock caught my eye as it rolled over to ten o'clock. That didn't make sense. It was just past sunset when I left town. How could I have lost so much time? I pounded the steering wheel in frustration as I spun the car around.

I pulled out my phone, put it on speaker, and listened with growing dread as Leon's number continued to ring. I flicked the high beams off-and-on hoping it might catch Leon's attention. My ears thundered with the gushing of my own blood as it pounded through my veins. The hairs on my arms bristled as my mind leapt to the seedy plots in all those true-crime novels I'd devoured in more innocent moments on the road.

There was still no sign of Leon.

Frustration pushed its way toward panic. A part of me screamed to throw in the towel, to quit that very instant and head home to my wife and son. But I couldn't do it. Leon was miserable company and I only just tolerated him, but he was my partner. We'd suffered together, and I knew despite our harsh words, he would never leave me behind. I was all he had.

I laid on the accelerator and the engine growled to life. Moths flicked through the high beams as I picked up speed.

I rolled down my window. "Leon!" I screamed, honking the horn. "Leon! Come on, man, where are you?" My voice died into the darkness of the cotton fields.

I was approaching the turnoff for the town again when suddenly my headlights caught a dark mass in front of me. I hit the brakes, but it was too late. There was a sickening thud as the thing I hit rolled up the hood of the car and crashed into the windshield.

Shock gripped me as the thing tumbled to the pavement. I could just make it out through the web of shattered glass. The form was too big to be a man, but in the spotlight of my headlights, I could see it was still alive. Its broken wings shuddered uselessly as it heaved, and a phosphorous green glow pulsated from beneath its crumpled form. The light grew and died in time to the trilling of my phone. When I retrieved it from down between my feet and closed the cover, the light beneath the creature went out. I would have to get out and look to be sure.

The door alarm chimed behind me as I crept along the asphalt. My shadow reached the crumpled form long before I did. When it fell across the matted black fur of the body, the shuddering ceased.

"Hello?" My voice cracked in my throat.

I stepped closer. When I stretched out my arm, words escaped in a garbled growl from beneath the black fur.

"Stay back."

"Are—are you alright?"

"Stay back!"

The voice was clear this time.

"Leon! God, Leon! What have they done to you?" I rushed forward, dropping to my knees. My hands hovered over the massive wings, unsure of where I should place them. "How do I get this thing off you?"

The wings shook as sobs emanated from beneath the fur.

"Leon, tell me what to do." I rested a tentative palm on the joint of the wing. The feathers were damp, and when I pulled my hand away, I saw my fingers were coated with amber goo. "Oh God," I whispered. "Leon, I think you're bleeding. We need to get you to a hospital."

I went to help him up, but as I reached his body he began to convulse. I scuttled backward as he lumbered to his feet, the wings stretching outward.

My scream stuck in my throat when I looked to where his face should be—a swarm of wriggling iridescent flies crawled over each other as their hissing increased to a buzz.

"Go! Run!" Leon's voice gurgled as he tried to shout. Awkwardly, the form stumbled toward me and the voice changed to a whining drone. "What are you looking at?!"

I scrambled to my feet and bolted toward the car. I dove head first into the driver's seat, slamming the door behind me. In the fractured windshield, I saw the thing writhing in the middle of the road, thrashing this way and that, as if it were battling some unseen foe. I revved the engine and hesitated as the undulating mask that was Leon's face went still. The iridescent bodies parted, revealing a glimpse of pink skin and human eyes that begged for salvation.

I threw the car into drive and slammed my foot on the gas. The tires squealed, and once again there was a sickening thud as the thing bounced off the bumper. I didn't look back as I sped away, the car fishtailing until I regained control. I couldn't look again.

Tears flowed hot and free until I reached the next exit and turned the car in the direction that would take me home. All I could hope was that the battered sedan would hold out until daylight, until I reached some semblance of civilization. I felt a tickle on my fingertips. I looked down, and by the light of the dashboard, saw a fly crest the knuckles of my right hand where it gripped the steering wheel. I slapped at it and nearly lost control of the car. A minute later, I looked again and saw that a red bump had formed.

What the Mirrors Keep
by Erin Cole

It all started on the night of the housewarming dinner, when my best friend Ted and his wife Sarah had come over for dinner to see our new house. It was the cusp of normal times, when relationships were healthy and friendships were strong, but something dark had pervaded Ted's thoughts that night, and it muted him for most of the evening.

He drew me outside to the deck for a drink, likely intending to tell me about it.

"House looks great," he said. "Classic, although I pegged you as being more modern." I had never known Ted to care about home décor.

"What's up with you?" I said. "You've barely spoken a word tonight."

Ted clinked the ice in his drink and spoke in a deep, husky voice. His serious voice.

"Tell me, Paul, are you happy? I mean, really happy?"

Ted had always been at odds with Janelle. She was different from other woman: quiet, graceful, keenly ambitious, didn't like the word no. Ted had confronted me once, saying that love didn't pull you away from others; it was supposed to bring you closer to them. I'd always thought he was jealous, and it was never more obvious than that night.

"What kind of question is that? Sure, I'm happy."

His gaze crossed the patio and landed somewhere behind me, in the kitchen. "So you and the kids are doing okay?" When his eyes slid back to mine, they were full of need.

"We have our usual ups and downs."

Not liking the direction of our conversation, I poured another splash of scotch into my tumbler. I wasn't in the mood to dig up old bones I thought we had buried years ago. Ted extended his glass and I filled it. We both swilled a gulp in silence. Ted averted his attention to the stars above us. Whatever troubled him was bound to escape.

"I know there's something you want to say, so say it."

Ted lifted his drink to his mouth and paused, as if articulating the best defense.

Impatience rattled my nerves. "For Christ's sake, what the Hell is it?"

The words popped from Ted's mouth like a cork. "I saw something in Janelle. Something's not right about her."

I couldn't believe we were facing this problem again. "You saw something in Janelle? What on God's green Earth are you talking about?"

He leaned in toward me, eyeing the kitchen window behind us. Janelle and Sarah were still cleaning up the table. "I don't know exactly."

I thought for a half-breath that he might be high. We used to smoke weed in college, but that was two decades ago, and Ted was a firefighter now.

"What exactly did you see?" I asked, working to remain calm and levelheaded.

Ted shifted on his feet like an embarrassed teenager. "I passed by Janelle's study the other day when I was over here helping you move the hutch. She was standing in front of a mirror, talking. I saw something in it." He pinned me down with an expression that cooled the air around me. "I saw a reflection that wasn't hers."

We had also pulled off a few practical jokes in college, including one that landed us in the slammer, but again, that was behavior from pot-smoking college days.

"Ah, good one." I laughed. "You almost had me that time." Ted wasn't chuckling or even smiling. My laughter faded like fogged breath. I returned to his ridiculous remark with added frustration. "What do you mean it wasn't her reflection?"

I gulped the rest of my drink in a burning-hot swig I hoped would drown my unease, because I didn't want to hear his answer. The sliding glass door scraped open. Sarah poked her head outside.

"Ted, I'm not feeling well. Do you mind if we leave early?"

Ted eyed me again with a look less comforting than a punch to the gut. No, he definitely wasn't high or joking. Genuine fear showed in his face.

"I'll be right there." He walked to the door and turned to me. "Keep in touch."

♦

"She doesn't like me," Janelle said after Ted and Sarah drove off. She gazed at them through a small split in the curtain. From where I stood, I could see a slice of her face reflected in the window—her face, not another reflection—and it was just as young and beautiful as the day we were married.

"I don't think that's true," I lied. I didn't have the heart to tell her that I didn't think Ted liked her, either. Somehow, I gathered that she already knew.

S

A few nights later, our son Luke padded into our bedroom, crying. His body was shaking uncontrollably as if he'd been standing in cold rain for hours.

"What's wrong, pal?" I said as I rubbed both of my hands up and down his arms.

"Something was talking to me in my room."

"Talking to you? Where? From the window?" He and our daughter Madeline shared a room. My thoughts detoured into darkness. "Is the window open? Is Madeline still in her bed?"

Luke tried to quiet me with a sweeping gesture of his hand. "Yeah, she's asleep. It was in the mirror. Something was in the mirror."

Janelle lifted her head. "It was probably just a bad dream, honey. Be a big boy and go back to bed. We'll talk about it in the morning."

I walked Luke back to his room and tucked his red race-car comforter around his shoulders. I caressed his head until his eyes shut.

Then I walked over to the mirror. I stepped in front of it and peered into it up close. My mind said that monstrous hands were about to jet out of it, snatch me by the shoulders, and jerk me inside it, or at least materialize another face, not my own.

I saw nothing, just my own weary reflection. I went back to bed.

◆

We never did talk about the mirror the next morning. Luke didn't bring it up, but something had changed in him. I recalled the strange conversation with Ted regarding the reflection he claimed to have seen in the mirror. Had Luke seen something similar?

I found both incidents too bizarre for further consideration and carried on as if nothing had happened.

A few nights later, the mirror went missing from the wall in Luke and Madeline's bedroom.

"What happened to the mirror?" I asked Luke, standing in the middle of his and Madeline's room.

He looked over at Madeline, her eyes shut and attention lost to the headphones tethered to her mp3 player. He brought his finger to his mouth and pointed under his bed.

I bent down on hands and knees and peered underneath the bed frame. A mess of lost toys and missing socks cluttered the dark space. In the back corner, something bright and silver gleamed. Tinfoil.

"You wrapped the mirror in tinfoil?"

He signaled again for me to keep quiet. "It's the only way to block its reflection," he whispered.

"It?"

"The thing in the mirror."

He had a familiar look in his eyes, the same one as in Ted's. I wouldn't say then that monstrous hands out of nowhere had indeed grasped me, but it sure as Hell felt as if something was pulling me into a nightmare.

♦

Madeline and Luke battled incessantly over the bedroom mirror. When Luke wasn't around, she stole it back from beneath his bed and strung it over the nail on the wall, but as soon as she left the room, Luke took it back down, wrapped it up in tinfoil again, and shoved it back under his bed. After that, he hid it in the mattress, the dresser, and finally, the bathroom closet. Janelle stopped buying tinfoil.

I did everything I could to placate Luke's preoccupation with the mirror except talk with Ted, a conversation I didn't want to have.

He came by the house one evening, oddly refusing to come inside, saying something about a cold he didn't want to pass on to the kids. *Bullshit*, I thought. I found Ted's new aloof nature a bit bothersome.

I told him about Luke and the mirror, cringing at what he might or might not say next.

Ted crossed his arms when I finished. "What do you want me to say?"

"I want you to tell me the truth. What's really bothering you?"

"I did tell you the truth, and you laughed. Remember?"

"What did you see in the mirror, Ted? I've got Luke saying the same—" A thought slipped into my mind like a thorn. No, no, he didn't ... he wouldn't ... "Have you already spoken to Luke about this? Did you tell him what you saw?"

"No. C'mon, I wouldn't do that."

"Then what's going on?!" Anger blew an ill wind through me.

Ted pointed at the house. "It's her." His voice fell flat against the stucco siding, or maybe it was the wall forming between us.

I glanced around the side of the house, making sure Janelle was still in the backyard, gardening.

"You've never liked Janelle," I protested in a heated whisper. "Just admit it."

I felt like berating Ted, because given a few more seconds' thought, I realized it came down to envy, plain and simple. There was no other explanation. Ted was jealous of what I had achieved in business, of who I had married, and even of the kids I'd had when he and Sarah couldn't conceive. Something red and hot worked itself inside me.

"We both made our own decisions," I stammered.

Ted lowered his head. "We've been friends for a long time. I'll be honest with you, even if you don't like it."

"Then stop trying to turn this on me. After all the times I helped you and Sarah—"

"Janelle is a demon, Paul."

The word "demon" hit me like a punch between the eyes—worse, actually, because it didn't stop at my skull. It bore through bone and brain and sank into my heart. I couldn't believe what he had just said. *He must be crazy*, I thought. That was it. He'd gone mad, and I didn't want any part of it. I turned around and headed for the front door without saying a word.

"I'm as serious about this as I've ever been about anything in my life," Ted said.

"You're insane, then." I kept walking. *Fucking insane.*

Ted stopped me at the screen door. "I have something to give you." He held out his hand. "I want Luke to have this."

It was a gold-plated medal, the one awarded to him last year for going "above and beyond the call of duty" at a Level-4 fire at the mill. Ted had lost one of his buddies that day. Emotion squeezed at my throat.

"What are you doing, Ted? I don't understand. What's wrong with you?"

"Just take it, please, and tell Sarah—" Ted broke off with a jerk of his head.

The sweet scent of jasmine drifted at my side. Janelle had come from the backyard, shears in her gloved hand, with a star-gleaming smile and blue eyes like glacial ice.

"Hi, Ted. I didn't even know you were here. You want to come inside for some iced tea?"

"No thanks." He turned to me. "I'd better get back to the station."

I watched him drive off and roll through the stop sign ahead.

"What's that?" Janelle asked, pointing to my hand. She approached me with an intense, quizzical stare.

"Just something Ted wanted me to give to Luke."

"Well, that was nice of him, but I don't think we should accept it."

"Why?"

A malicious frown curled from Janelle's mouth and into her eyes. "I don't think our son should accept gifts from a man who peeps in on his best friend's wife while she's changing. We should call him Peeping Ted."

Janelle's comment upset me. I couldn't believe that I thought for even a half-second that Ted would do such a thing. Then I reasoned that Janelle sensed Ted's dislike for her, so she made the situation into something it wasn't.

◆

None of it mattered anymore.

The following morning, Sarah found Ted on the bathroom floor, his eyes frozen open toward the ceiling. Reports said his blood pressure had dropped too low and he had died in his sleep.

"All those years of smoke inhalation and steady stress," the coroner remarked.

The problem with the conclusion was where Ted had died. He had no bruising or head injury from tripping or falling, so unless he had been drinking heavily or sleepwalking—two things he didn't do—it didn't make any sense why he would be on the bathroom floor.

I couldn't ignore the persistent thought that something else had happened to him. Given his unusual behavior the days before, I had to wonder if he'd done something to himself. Then another thought crested and crashed: *What if Janelle did something? What if she was ... ?*

The thought was outrageous. Stuff for B movies, not an event in my life. But the thought that Janelle might not be what she seemed continued to fester in my thoughts over the next few days.

♦

At Ted's funeral, Luke wept beside an oak tree. Ted had treated him like a nephew. I tried to talk to Luke, but he wouldn't open up to his mother or me. When Janelle wasn't looking, I handed him the medal Ted had given me. Luke knew who it belonged to; he had been at the award ceremony.

"Ted told me he wanted you to have this."

Luke nodded. A plump tear rolled down his cheek. He hung the medal around his neck and slipped it inside his shirt.

Madeline immersed herself in one of those tabloid gossip magazines during the eulogy. I wanted her to show some respect, so I took it from her.

She spent the next two days pretending I didn't exist. Janelle said it was what preteens did and that I was being too hard on her, letting my grief surpass my judgement. I silently disagreed with her, an increasingly common occurrence. Every day, I climbed further up the wall that had formed between Ted and me. I wondered if one day I would jump over to his side, opposite from Janelle.

♦

Luke grew more distant. Unlike Madeline, he slipped in and out of dark, silent moods and sank further into isolation. He reinstated his mission with the mirrors, this time taking all of them down. Madeline shouted her complaints to Janelle. Janelle cornered Luke before dinner one night.

"The mirrors are important for a girl's self-image, Luke, and if you don't stop taking them down, I'm going to have them permanently mounted above your bed."

"Don't talk to him like that," I said, grabbing Janelle by the arm. I had never spoken or touched her like that before. I let go of her arm, and the white outline of my fingers darkened to red across her skin. "He's still grieving," I added, ashamed of my outburst.

She conceded and pointed a crimson-painted fingernail at my chest. "Fine. But the mirror in my study stays."

♦

Over the next few weeks, I strived to rekindle my father-son bond with Luke. He never discussed the mirrors with me, and I didn't want to bring up anything that might jeopardize our rocky relationship.

Still, at night, just before dozing off in those weightless spaces of pre-sleep, I knew something was amiss with Janelle, a feeling that deepened each day. Madeline, too. A mark on their souls, maybe, and for the first time, I began to see things from Ted's perspective, noticing the dark side of Janelle she concealed from the rest of the world.

One night, I woke to an empty bed after a nightmare that had formed around Ted's last comment regarding Janelle. Outside the window, the fog had folded in so tight I couldn't see the bordering pines. It played on my tension.

I heard voices streaming down the hall from Janelle's study. Not like those spoken by people, but a crackling muffle as if it were coming through a radio.

I crept down the hall, up to the door, and inched my head around the corner. I caught the edge of movement, Janelle's soft, petite elbow, and the wave of her robe. A little bit further and I could see her standing before the mirror, speaking. At first, I imagined it was to herself, but my thoughts replayed what both Luke and Ted had said. It wasn't Janelle's reflection. Something was talking to me in the mirror.

The scrape of a footstep from behind startled me. I jerked around.

"Dad? What are you doing?"

"Shit, Madeline, you scared me." I moved away from the door and against the wall where Janelle couldn't see us.

"Are you spying on Mom?"

"No, of course not." I cinched my robe tighter, pretending the chill was to blame for my jitters.

"You know she doesn't like Peeping Teds."

My body froze before my mind could assimilate exactly what it was she'd said. I reeled inside.

"Watch your mouth, young lady." How could Janelle have told her that?

It was at that moment that I jumped over Ted's wall, and both Madeline and Janelle were on the other side.

"What?" Madeline said, feigning innocence with a smile becoming more like her mother's every day, enigmatic and knowing.

The door to Janelle's office creaked open. She stepped out,

hugging the door tight against herself as if there were a dog inside that shouldn't escape.

"What are you two doing?"

"Dad was spying on you, and I'm hungry."

Janelle's eyes slid over to me.

"I wasn't spying," I replied. "I couldn't sleep and came to find you."

"Well, now you found me." She squeezed past the door, shut it behind her, and passed by me without a glance, taking Madeline under her arm. I heard them talking in the kitchen, speaking in an incomprehensible low tone, to be a fly on the other side of my wall.

♦

Luke fell ill. At first, we thought he had a cold or a mild case of the flu, but then he sank into deep sleeps during the day and had lost most of his appetite. I couldn't even get him to eat his favorite cereal.

We took him to the doctors, had him examined, and ran blood tests, but nobody could figure out what was wrong with him. I sat by his bed every chance I could, sticking Ted's medal beneath his pillow for good measure. I wasn't religious, but somehow I hoped Ted would watch over him.

That night, his fever spiked. I patted his face and chest with a wet washcloth. He rolled and shifted uncomfortably in his bed, muttering and moaning. I struggled to hear his slurred words, crushed under the heavy heat of his sickness. Then one audible word escaped from him and clanged against my heart like a cymbal: "Mirror."

The accumulation of events over the last two months awakened me with a clear, definitive resolution. I knew what needed to be done. Maybe I had known all along but lacked the desperation to act until then.

Janelle and Madeline were sleeping soundly. I walked quietly down the hall and into Janelle's study. The baseball bat weighed heavy in my hand. The mirror on the wall that Janelle made me promise me not to touch, the one that Ted had seen the reflection in, hung in the far corner.

It looked older than I remembered: a square teak-and-maple border with intricate carvings too detailed to see clearly in the darkened room, oval-shaped and beveled at the edge, the way they used to craft them centuries ago, with a splotchy film covering it from oxidation over time.

I approached it as though it were a sleeping bear, heeding the worm-like sensation writhing in my gut. Filtered green light reflected in the mirror even though there wasn't a green bulb or lamp in the room. I edged closer, looking at it from the side, too intimidated to stand directly in front of it. Monstrous hands emerging didn't seem far-fetched at all.

Then, ever so subtly, a shadow flitted inside the mirror. Instinctively, I spun around. Nobody was there. I looked back into the mirror, stepped closer, almost at arm's length, and waited against the silence of the house. I shifted my head a fraction of an angle when a figure emerged from the mirror with astonishing speed.

It jolted me backward. My mind turned on itself as I stared at what peered back at me. My breath wheezed in fitful gasps as I fought for air. I didn't, couldn't comprehend what I was seeing.

A hideous thing, with rope-veined skin pulled tight over grotesque bulges, bulges that weren't just bones. Teeth like claws. A pointed, black tongue and yellow, burning eyes.

Evil. A demon.

It spoke to me, told me Luke was going to die, told me it had killed Ted, and said that I was next.

I wrenched myself from its madness and clenched the bat as tight as I could. Putting all my strength into one blow, I swung at the mirror. A high-pitched wail screeched out. Hot, white pain stabbed into my head and forced me to drop the bat. It clanged to the floor. I curled up on the floor and pressed my palms over my ears. Pain seared into me.

I glimpsed movement and looked up. The thing in the mirror leaned forward, seemingly ready to climb out. In one last desperate attempt—for Luke, for Ted—I lunged for the bat and hurled it at the mirror, smashing it against the glass.

A crack splintered out from the center like a broken blood vessel. Shards of glass popped from the frame and shattered to the floor in jagged, angular pieces. Seconds later, a scream exploded from upstairs.

I ran out of the study, following the cry into my bedroom. Madeline stood beside our bed, mouth agape in horror. Janelle had turned a sickly purple as if she couldn't breathe. I crouched over her and administered pumps to her sternum.

"Madeline! Call an ambulance!"

My lips molded around Janelle's. I lifted her neck up and blew breath inside her mouth, then worked her chest again.

"Janelle! Janelle!"

I shook her limp form.

Oh God, Janelle.

♦

They took her away just as dawn broke, gold across pewter clouds. The coroner said she died of heart complications. Madeline wouldn't speak to me or anyone else.

Minutes after Janelle's death, Luke had climbed from his bed, pale and gaunt, but alive. When he looked at me, we both knew, understanding that darkness lived in the mirrors.

The following morning, I found Madeline in Janelle's study. She was picking up shards of the mirror and attempting to piece them back into the maple-carved frame.

"Madeline, honey? What are you doing?"

"Putting it back together." She picked up another shard of glass and looked into it. "It's all I have left of Mother."

Golden Arms

by Joshua Mannix

Matthew concentrates as he rolls his new arms in front of his eyes. They're still skin-colored, as he had requested, but with no marks, moles, scars, or hair, smooth as a baby's skin. The bulk that his old arms had possessed, the bulk that only earned silver, is present but streamlined.

He flexes his artificial muscles, grips his fists together, and stretches his arms wide. He expects to hear gears turning beneath the skin, like in movies, but nothing makes a sound. The eeriest aspect of seeing the arms in front of him, attached to his shoulders with thin lines indicating where they had made the cut, is that he can't feel them at all.

"That numbness will be around for a couple of weeks as the nerves connect to the circuits." Dr. Harrison pokes Matthew's hands with a needle. If he hadn't watched the point press into the synthetic skin, he wouldn't have known it was there. "Make sure you're keeping an eye on where they go."

"Yeah, of course." The doctor chuckles to himself at his joke, but Matthew stares at the foreign limbs without cracking a smile. He sees his hands form a fist in front of him the second after he wills it, but doesn't feel the tight clench of strength. "How long till I can get these babies working?"

"A few weeks at best, for basic control, but probably a month or two for more intricate use." Dr. Harrison grabs a computer tablet from the end of the bed and pokes at the screen. "You'll experience some pain while that happens, a sharp tingling that feels like you slept on it wrong, or itching along your arms that won't go away."

"Great, a few weeks of walking around with arms I have to concentrate a hundred percent on to do anything." Matthew's face scrunches together as he lifts his arms up over his head.

"The pain will be good sign, but along with the pain, you'll be feeling your phantom limbs until the connection solidifies. But hey!" The doctor slaps Matthew's shoulder, though he can't feel it. "In a month, you'll be back to doing what you do best!"

The word "best" makes Matthew grit his teeth. He tightens his fists without meaning to and rolls his shoulders to get them to relax. With the new arms, he will be the best, unlike with the old ones that failed him. His father told him a long time ago, when he was still learning weightlifting in high school, that there were no excuses, no runners up, and only one winner. Words to live by. Matthew looks down at his new, more powerful arms, and thinks that today is the first step toward gold.

"Where are my old arms?" He didn't expect to say the words, but the thought struck him and they rolled out before he could stop.

"They are—" The doctor checks the watch that Matthew is surprised he wears. "—about to be incinerated."

"Is it possible that I can—"

"Go say a farewell?" He smiles, having heard the line hundreds of times. "Of course, let me call down to the morgue."

"Thank you," Matthew says without correcting the doctor. The arms had always been weak, broke when he needed them to work, and lost him a championship that he had been working toward all of his life. He never looked at them the same after that, instead growing envious of the other competitors who were going with the trend of artificial limbs. He isn't going to be saying farewell.

Dr. Harrison comes back into the room and removes the IV line that was attached to Matthew's thigh and the heart monitor clips from his barrel-sized chest. "All set. They are lying out there, waiting for you. Do you know where to go?"

"I'm sure I can follow a few signs." He tosses his legs over the side of the bed and plants them on the cold tile floor. He wobbles a bit from the painkillers coursing through his body.

"Down the hall, elevator to the basement floor, fourth door on the right." Dr. Harrison says, opening the door.

In the hallway, doctors and nurses walk by with charts in their hands. Other patients meander, rolling their IVs next to them. Matthew is wearing the stereotypical hospital gown with the back showing his ass, but he doesn't care. It is colder in the hallway than in his room, and the odd feeling of his body being cold, but not his arms, sets in.

He rubs his neck to warm it up, trying to ignore the absence of sensation in his hand. The new hand is warm, however. He thought it would be like an ice cube on first touch, but a soothing sensation settles across the back of his neck. He looks down to get a better angle for the hand. In that instant, he sees his arms hanging slack, unmoving.

His eyes widen in frustration as the phantom limb rubs against his neck. He concentrates to get the feeling away, lifting his senseless arms, getting it into his mind that they are his limbs now. A mist of nervous sweat forms across his neckline. How often will he have to be reminded of his failed arms?

He keeps his artificial ones moving up and down, like he is lifting weights at the gym, during the entire walk toward the elevator. He clicks the basement button and a red circle appears around it, a good thing, or he wouldn't have been able to know if he hit it hard enough.

When he steps out of the elevator, he sees his breath float in front of his face. He specifically thinks not to rub his neck like he did upstairs, double-checking his arms to make sure they're hanging still. The floor is mostly deserted, but a few coroners are in their separate rooms, typing on computers or examining bodies that Matthew turns his head away from. On the fourth door on the right, a placard reads

"Depository."

The room is wall-to-wall medium-sized boxes, each one of them silver with a little white tag on the front describing what's inside. On the right side of the room, a black square is set into the wall, with two buttons on the side, red and green. The smell of fire and cooked flesh emanate from it. An incinerator.

A table in the middle of the room takes up most of the walking area. Reflecting silver like the storage boxes, it sits under the single large light adorning the ceiling. At the edge of the table, his old arms stare at him through a vacuum-sealed bag, like a lost lover.

The bag makes them look out of focus, smearing any characteristics that were painted on, reminding Matthew of his new arms, smooth and featureless. He runs his hand over the bag, feeling nothing but imagining the smooth texture of the material. He grits his teeth again, annoyed at the sight of his old arms imitating his new, stronger ones. It takes him a moment of concentration to grip the plastic bag, then rip it open.

The smell of formaldehyde hits his nose as he folds the plastic back. The thick arms, littered with memories, fit like shoes in the wrapping. He spreads his artificial hand over the old one, comparing the size. They are the same; the designers did a damn fine job replicating them.

He grabs the preserved right hand in a handshake, gripping hard, hard enough to hear the bones start to crack from the force. His synthetic hands compress tighter at his will, and the snap of the bones breaking makes a smile curve along his cheek. He lifts the arm up, knowing he made the right choice. The new ones are a hurricane compared to a breeze.

But something shines out of place on his old arm. A slender scar trails from the wrist and fades at the elbow. Jack Lunster, the name comes to mind, the kid who tried to stab him back in high school. He almost got the drop on Matthew, sneaked up from behind after he left the school's weight room. At the last second, the sound of Jack's footsteps made Matthew whip around to see him swinging a knife at his back. Matthew blocked the quick slice through the air with his right arm and knocked the bastard out with a left counterpunch. He can't remember why Lunster had wanted to attack him. Probably something he said. He shrugs it off.

Adjacent to the knife scar is a wide blotch of dark red skin shaped like an exploding firework. The hair never grew back after grease had splattered there from his first job as a fry cook. His father had told him to get working as a 16th birthday present. When the grease splashed on him, he yelled at the top of his lungs as the skin disintegrated down to the muscle. Customers from the front of the restaurant heard him and asked if someone was dying in the back—only after they had asked about their food, of course. Once a few minutes passed of Matthew trembling from the pain, his coworkers laughed it off with him, the first of many they said, showing him their own burn marks. They wrapped gauze around it and he finished his shift with the help of a small bottle of whiskey that the manager kept around for such incidents.

Now, remembering one of his favorites, he picks up the left arm, looking at his fingers. The ring finger is bent slightly to the right. When he first started to get serious about weightlifting, he didn't have an instructor, just a pre-recorded online video. When he tried a snatch, lifting the barbell from the ground to above his head in one single motion, he unbalanced himself and the whole barbell rolled out of his hands, falling behind him. His ring finger, the last to hold on, stretched back, almost touching the back of his hand, and snapped like a tree branch. A gym instructor found him holding a scream in his mouth. He called an ambulance and then an old weightlifter friend of his, to help Matthew start his career.

The only tattoo on his body stuck out to him now: on his left shoulder, an emblem from the Army division he had joined, two red bayonets across a blue field. Good times in those years, post-training football games, weekend leave into the city for some fun, more than he can remember now. Bad times also, things he wanted to forget but couldn't, like Marcus Ruben dying in combat, the nights of eyes pried open by paranoia, the heat of the summers. He shakes off the bad memories that won't fade into the past and drops the arm onto the table.

"Weak bastards," He says as he opens and closes his new hand. "You couldn't win me gold, but these will."

Blank slate, some philosopher said, that's where he is now. No more silver, no more second place. Damn all the memories that he had with his old arms. He can easily make new ones, and the next memory will be of the sweet taste of victory, standing on the highest podium with gold draped around his neck. Matthew starts walking toward the door, glad to get those shameful arms out of his sight once and for all. Before he grabs the knob to pull the door open, a force from nowhere wraps like a noose around his neck.

The first gasp of breath is from surprise. There hadn't been anyone in the room besides Matthew. The second gasp is from not getting air into his lungs. Panic sets in, and he tries to flail his arms at whoever is strangling him, but encounters nothing behind his back. He twists and turns his whole body, trying a jiu-jitsu move to throw the person off, but no weight falls across his back. His knees drop to the tile floor, the lack of air making his head foggier than it was already.

He turns to at least try and see the person who will kill him. Only the detached arms greet his eyes from a few feet away. They are turned to face Matthew now, somehow moving on their own, fingers outstretched like claws digging into flesh. For a moment, the tightening stranglehold around his neck is forgotten, and the only thought that beats in his head is disbelief at what is happening. Then the pain kicks back in, pain from his former arms that are somehow crushing his windpipe without touching it.

Golden Arms

Matthew stands to one leg, lungs starving for relief, and leaps back to the metal table, knocking his head against the outstretched severed arms. His tongue is shaking hard, trying to mouth a shout or shovel air into his chest. He grabs the arms, concentrating to keep them in his grip, and stumbles over to the incinerator. Willing his numb hand to grasp the handle, he yanks open the furnace, revealing a charred black interior.

With his right arm, he tosses both of his old arms inside, their fingers still rigid, throttling with their invisible strength. Matthew slams his whole shoulder against the green button as he kicks up the door, slamming it shut. Fire roars into life on the other side of the metal container, and even through its shielding, he can feel the heat.

The vice grip on his neck disappears, leaving only a bruised ache. He coughs before taking a deep breath. His new hands are black with the soot from the incinerator. A stray thought pounds against his mind like a prisoner wanting free, though he doesn't know why it is there, "Are we strong enough?"

Fostering

by Loren Eaton

Before Theresa even opened her eyes, she knew the rain had stopped. The air hung still and silent, devoid of the near-ceaseless pattering that skittered over her roof in the cold months. She knew that the gray dawn sky would soon be filled with gaggles of geese. She knew squirrels would stir from their winter nests.

She also knew that it wouldn't let Richard lie still.

Theresa pushed an arm over to his side of the bed, felt the rumpled sheets, cold but still smelling faintly of Ivory soap, baby shampoo, a trace of male musk—his scent. He was scheduled to work today, but not this early. She threw back the covers, hoping against hope to find him enjoying another cup of coffee, running an iron over his Bochsler True Value polo, polishing a pair of loafers rather than lacing up those scarred old work boots …

But no. The door to the hall closet hung open, the Ruger .22 rifle and orange hunting vest that were normally inside were now missing. Glancing out the front window, she confirmed that the Chevy was gone too.

Later, as she scraped her plate clean of scraps of her bean-sprout omelet, she discovered an empty break-and-bake biscuit container in the trash, 8.4 grams of fat per serving. Disgusting.

"I know he'd never raise a hand against me," Theresa told the sink, which held dirty dishes haphazardly stacked against a greasy cookie sheet. Yes, but he would also never allow prior obligations to come between himself and a romp through the woods on a clear day, even when it wasn't hunting season, would he? She sighed. But honestly, why bother getting angry at his habits? She was certainly used to them.

The tins of loose chamomile and rooibos were almost empty, but the back of the cupboard yielded some Darjeeling. Theresa typically drank herbal, but tea of any kind was her constant comfort, and the caffeine boost wouldn't hurt considering all she had to do around their almost-working farm today. The ducks needed to be let out of the hutch, the compost turned, and the pasture's wire fence checked for breaks, all of it done completely on her own.

The work coat hung loosely about her narrow shoulders as she shrugged into it. The air that swirled around her when she shoved open the service porch's swinging door held the promise of frost if only the mercury would fall a few more degrees. Winter in Marion County was something she couldn't have imagined growing up in Tennessee, a season of fits and starts, always teasing with snow and only putting out sun-shrouding rain. But she'd gotten used to it. Fourteen years could do that.

Theresa trudged around the side of their two-story colonial, noting in her mind the wan, yellow paint peeling in patches, the grass, nearly gray in the gloom, and the distant evergreens cutting a dark line across the horizon. The chain-link gate by the back field shrieked as she pushed it open, hanging crooked on its hinges. Another chore.

Then, down where the blackberry bushes surrendered to sheep-cropped grass, she saw the bright splashes of blood on the turf.

♦

"Dunno what did it. Dog, maybe wolf." Collins shook his head at the mangled forms lying before him in the pasture.

"The llama normally keeps things like that away. That why we got it." Theresa looked at the collar of Collins's frayed flannel shirt, the other sheep frisking in the field, and the layers of clouds pushed about by high-altitude winds, anywhere but the remains of dark organ meat spilling from the dead ewe or the pink nub of spine protruding from the lamb's headless neck.

Collins harrumphed. "Whatever it was, it ate the Hell out of them both."

"I don't think they belonged to each other." She pointed a few yards off to where a ewe was aiming a kick at a lamb nuzzling her udders. "See? That's why I called. Richard once said that you know everything about sheep. If she won't let it nurse, she'll get … I can't remember what it's called."

"Mastitis," Collins said. "Don't worry, we'll have her fostering that lamb right quick."

"Fostering? How?"

Collins patted his belt, and Theresa noticed for the first time the knife sheathed there.

"You, uh, may not want to watch this," he said, bending over the lamb's corpse.

♦

Speckled legs pistoned in Theresa's grasp.

"Easy," Collins said. "Lemme finish with the twine and—there!"

With a spastic twitch, the lamb thrust itself away and trotted off a dozen yards.

Collins wiped his hands on stained Carhartts. "It's all in the smell. Give it 24 hours and that ewe'll think she birthed him. Good for both of them." He pointed at the lamb. "Know what we call what he's wearing? A dinner jacket."

The sheath of hide covered the lamb from forelimbs to neck and around its back, a coverlet rimmed with ghastly pink and cinched tight by cord sewn up the front, as neat as any surgeon's stitching.

"Why?" Theresa asked.

Laughter roared out of Collins. "He won't get any dinner without it! And that—" He pointed at the two loops of twine about the lamb's throat. "—that's his bow tie!"

Theresa lifted her lips in approximation of a smile.

♦

When Theresa tried to press the bills into Collins's hand, he pushed them away. "I live half a mile away, and I'm a bachelor," he said. "No trouble at all. Call whenever."

Not long after he left, the rain began again.

She steeped the rest of the chamomile and settled into the living-room couch, its ancient springs sagging under her 95 pounds. She was secretly glad Collins had refused the money. They needed it. She tracked every cent, because who knew? Maybe one day they could afford a trip someplace sunny, to Santa Barbara or Scottsdale or even Cancun. But the farm barely provided enough revenue to cover its expenses and some part of the house always needed fixing and Richard was hardly on the fast track for a promotion.

She reached for the newspaper she'd laid out on the coffee table to dry. She wasn't scheduled to work at the library for almost a week, couldn't keep working outside, and didn't want to walk a mile and a half in the damp to the bus stop. Mulling over money wouldn't make the day pass any faster, but at least the rain would bring Richard home quicker. Maybe.

She clicked on a table lamp and began to read the op-eds. When she finished with the business section, she picked up a three-week-old copy of *People*. When she finished with that, she started the Betty Neels novel she'd salvaged from a rummage sale and never got around to starting.

These days were always quiet. Richard refused to carry a cell phone, said they'd rot your brain. She'd gotten used to it. But when the sky began to darken, worry wormed its way into her gut.

Fostering

◆

Theresa was wondering for the umpteenth time whether or not to call the police when the front door jolted against its deadbolt. Her feet beat a fast tattoo on the floor as she raced to it, and her fingers slipped on the lock's tab twice before the bolt thudded back.

"Richard, where have you been? My goodness, you're *soaked*."

"I got lost. In the woods."

"You're dripping everywhere. Get in the shower and I'll heat up some soup."

"Not hungry. Just want to sleep."

"Richard."

A pause. "Yes?"

"That's the service porch. Bathroom's over here."

"Right. I'm just tired."

"Go on, then."

As she mopped the watery mess of the floor, Theresa noticed the smell, a marshy dampness, a mustiness mixed with sweet decay.

◆

The next morning, Richard begged off breakfast. He only wanted a glass of water and to go to work.

"It's Sunday," Theresa explained. "The hardware store's closed."

He stared at her, puzzled. "Then what am I supposed to do?"

What was he supposed to do? Normally, Theresa would've had a hundred replies ready and waiting. She'd gotten used to mentally cataloguing an endless list of unfinished tasks. But the question caught her so off-guard that she stammered the first thing that popped into her mind.

"Uh, well, the duck pen has a few loose boards that need nailing. I, um, could hold an umbrella while you work."

"Okay," Richard said, and he actually smiled.

It was good the task turned out to be simple, because it took Richard twice as long as it ought to. He mashed this thumb, used twice as many nails as needed and sent the ducks into a frenzy with his haphazard hammering. They cowered in the corner farthest from him even after he'd finished.

One task down, who knows how many more to go, thought Theresa. Still, it was something.

Then Richard said, "What next?"

Theresa was steadying a loose banister on the front porch steps when a bright wink of light from the front of the Chevy caught her eye.

"Oh, that," Richard said, noticing her gaze. "Brushed a tree trunk last night. I'll get it fixed."

"I see," she replied, noting the truck's pristine paint, the unblemished sweep of its bumper and a pocked hole no bigger than the tip of a pinky in the middle of what was once a headlight.

♦

The screech of a starter jerked Theresa from her sleep. She staggered to the front door where she saw the Chevy rattle its way down the gravel path that served as their driveway, stall once just past the gate, and finally lurch onto Route 213. A note in Richard's messier-than-usual chicken scratch hung from the refrigerator. It told her that he loved her and he'd left early for work and he hoped she'd have a good day. The clock above the stove read 6:47.

Theresa made her second cup of Darjeeling that week and, yawning, settled at the kitchen table, which no longer rocked. Through the kitchen window, she peered at a gap in the blackberry bushes and saw a pair of sheep down in the pasture, the small one snatching a moment at the udder before the large one moved off. Even at a distance, the hide sheath was visible. Some progress, then.

She boiled a bowlful of quinoa, adding cinnamon and a little milk. She hadn't gone to the grocery store in days, but the refrigerator seemed almost full. Odd. The rain had slackened to a drizzle, nothing a poncho couldn't keep out. She'd never gotten around to checking the fence, had she?

Down by the back gate, she found the ducks snapping in the grass for slugs, their feathers sodden. The door to the pen gaped, even though the latch was sound. Theresa counted the ducks as she corralled them, tallied them a second time and then a third. She couldn't make the numbers add up. Then she circled the overhanging oak by the edge of the garden where she discovered a spray of feathers and a filigree of crimson dappling the brown bark.

♦

The phone rang 17 times before a breathless voice answered, "It's a great day at Bochsler True Value."

"Craig, it's Theresa. I need to speak with Richard."

"He can't talk with you, of all people, right now."

"I'm not joking, it'll only take a—"

"I'm not joking either; it's insane here. What'd you do to him this weekend? His can-do attitude's great, but he barely seems to know the difference between a screwdriver and a circle saw. The boss has been smiling and screaming all morning. He's got him in the back office; I don't know what they've been talking about all this time."

"Fine. When he goes on break, tell him to give me a call, would you?"

Craig said he would, but a customer had just come in, gottogobye.

Not 30 seconds later, the phone jangled. It was the library, saying that Marianne had come down with stomach flu, and they knew it was short notice, but could Theresa take over her shifts for the next couple of days? Theresa said she could. Income was always welcome, and somewhere between scribbling down the specifics and finding the chronically misfiled bus schedule, she forgot entirely about the ducks.

♦

When they had both finished, Richard sighed, long and low. Theresa could feel herself smiling even after his breathing settled into a slow, steady rhythm. His willingness to please had been nice. Maybe her mother was wrong, maybe she hadn't married a child in man's clothing. She breathed in the scent of his sweat, musky and strangely sour.

She stared at the ceiling, listening to Richard's inhalations and exhalations. She counted the beats of her own heart. Then, realizing sleep wouldn't come anytime soon, she sat up and felt in the dark for her slippers.

Not a scrap of anything herbal remained in the tins, so Theresa made do with hot water and a squeeze of lemon, pacing as she sipped. Tomorrow she'd have to go into town for more tea. And maybe tomorrow they could finish planing the wood floor in the guest room so it didn't look like a set piece from *The Grapes of Wrath*. Maybe punctuality would mean a raise for Richard, and then they could then let the farm lie fallow or rent out the fields. Maybe—

Her foot turned sharply, painfully on something hard—one of Richard's loafers abandoned on the transition strip between the kitchen and living room. She cursed, reached to right it, and froze.

A splotch of red marred the edge of its heel, and a crushed bit of down was clinging to it.

When she eventually went back in bed, each hour slid by like tar. She was still awake when, sometime between midnight and dawn, the bed creaked and Richard's shadowy form rose from it.

Fostering

♦

Dawn came, gray as a charcoal drawing. The poncho Theresa wore did a decent job of keeping out the rain, but she could feel dampness creeping around the cuffs of her jeans and at the collar of her sweatshirt. In the gloom, the llama's excavated abdomen looked like a piece of baroque architecture, its exposed ribs rising out of the curves of stomach and liver, the coils of intestine.

She had just finished shaking out the poncho in the service porch when Richard cracked the door. He was already dressed, his khakis sharply creased, the Bochsler polo with nary a wrinkle.

"Morning," he said. "How'd you sleep?"

"Bad. Something got the llama."

Richard's brow furrowed. "Got it?"

"Killed it. Ate a lot of it."

"Huh."

"Won't be much fun burying something that size."

"I'll do it. Hey, don't you open the library today?"

She'd forgotten. "Ugh. What time is it?"

Richard told her. "Look," he said, "you'll be late if you take the bus. I'll drive you."

"But you'll have to skip breakfast. Don't wait, it would make me feel … uncomfortable."

"I want to. Plus I'm not really hungry."

He leaned in to kiss her. An odor of iron and salt washed over her.

She ducked her head, brushing by him. "Get the truck warmed up, then. I'll be right there."

Theresa hurried, she really did. Still, as she snagged her coat from the hall closet on the way out, she paused long enough to fumble for the Ruger, to eject its stubby, square magazine—and to count the seven shells it held, three shy of full capacity.

Outside, the Chevy's horn squawked.

◆

Theresa's punctuality ended up mattering little. For the first three hours, the only sounds that broke the silence were the tread of her shoes as she shelved books, the overhead fluorescents' humming, and her coworker Charlotte's congested snuffling.

Around 10:30, Mr. Bimsley hobbled in, clutching a history of Constantinople, a biography of Rita Hayworth, and a tattered paperback copy of *Westward the Tide*. Billy Cooper slunk over to the public computers at 11:47 to "check his email," and Theresa's administrator station tallied 23 attempts to circumvent the content filter before he logged off. At 1:03, Mrs. Hagglesmith deposited 17 overdue Harlequin romances on the checkout desk and chatted about her husband's colitis while she counted out the fine in pennies.

After that, the quiet returned.

"Hey, Char," Theresa said as the clock rounded two. "This place is dead and I've got some errands I really need to run. Will you cover for me?"

Charlotte's gaze played over the empty stacks, the deserted reading area, and the row of computer monitors all lit with the same floating, four-color square. She blew her nose and crumpled the tissue, adding it to the rising pyramid on the reference desk.

"Okay," she sniffed, "but you owe me."

The rain still fell as steadily as sand in an hourglass.

Theresa took the bus to the Roth's Fresh Market, where she bought tea, sausage, cheddar, eggs, a tube of ready-bake biscuits and a gallon of antifreeze. She double-knotted the plastic bags before trudging to the bus stop.

Back home, she dried off and made tea. The fostered lamb frolicked in the back field, its adoptive mother unperturbed when it ducked its head to nurse. Its dinner jacket had begun to pull free of the twine, the interior gray with decay. It would need to come off soon.

Fostering

She watched the pair for a long time. Then she drained her tea, picked up the antifreeze and went to find the shovel.

♦

When he got home, Richard didn't ask about dinner; he simply slunk into the shower. Theresa waited for the pipes to stop ticking and heard a muffled groan from the bedframe as it received his weight.

Then she started cooking.

Around midnight, the bedroom door eased open.

"Hello, honey," Theresa said.

Richard stared at the table laden with biscuits, sausage, and orange juice as though looking down the barrel of a gun.

"I made all your favorite junk foods," Theresa continued. "I thought you might be hungry, since you missed dinner. You are hungry, aren't you?"

He inclined his head up and down by the barest inch.

"Then pull up a chair. I'm just finishing up with the eggs."

He didn't move.

Theresa deposited a quivering mound of scrambled eggs on a plate and placed it by his spot at the table. "Is there a problem, sweetie?"

Richard cleared his throat. "There's, well, there's something I need to take care of."

"What would need attention this time of night? Certainly not the car. You shouldn't be embarrassed about that, sweetie. Hunting accidents happen, and a bullet through a headlight is easier to fix than a busted bumper."

The flatness in Richard's face made his smile ghastly. "Oh. That's good. Still, I'm going to step outside for a second—"

"In your underwear? By the way, I took care of the llama." She nodded toward the service porch. The empty bottle of antifreeze lay on its threshold. "Anything that digs it up will be sorry. So please, sit. Eat."

He didn't respond.

"It's what my husband would do," she said softly.

Richard opened his mouth to scream.

At least, that was what Theresa expected, but he gaped wider and wider, his mouth stretching beyond any dimension that could even vaguely be called human, his jaw popping as it unhinged. His hands curled in on themselves, suddenly boneless, his forearms dimpling as spines rose beneath the skin, his neck bulged, something maggot-white thrashed in the hole of his throat, and the kitchen flooded with the stench of methane and sour meat and old rot, freshly stirred—

"Stop." Theresa strived to keep the shaking out of her voice, to hold her ground. "I only … I need us to come to an understanding."

The thing that wore her husband's flesh hesitated.

Theresa swallowed and pressed on: "I understand this food isn't … isn't to your liking. You can't have our livestock, though. This has always been a working farm. People would notice." She hurried on. "But you keep doing well by me, and I'll do well by you. Listen."

Crossing the kitchen felt like slogging through quicksand. The phone's receiver seemed to weigh 50 pounds.

"Mr. Collins? I know it's late, but we lost more sheep, and Richard went out to check. He hasn't come back, and I'm scared. Oh, would you? In 15 minutes? That would mean so much."

The receiver rattled back into its cradle.

"Thank you." Her Richard stood before her again, flexing his fingers, working his jaw, his form restored once more. "You're different. From the others, I mean. I can see why he cared about you. He certainly fought like it."

The kitchen blurred behind a hot veil of tears. "Just … just go. And don't leave any—" She had to stop and swallow a sudden lump in her throat. "—any remains this time."

Fostering

Rain hammered on the roof. The smell lingered in the kitchen, so Theresa had scorched some tea leaves after making a cup for herself, hoping the burning would cover the stink. They'd have to do something about that. She'd have so much to adjust to. Finding him food, for one thing.

She already knew Collins and poor Billy Tindale, who lived near the dairy, but she should meet widow Johnson at some point and Robert Nordhaus, who did odd carpentry jobs out of his garage and maybe some of the residents at the Hopeview Mental Health Center. How long could they go without attracting notice? Six months? Nine months? A year, at most?

But if Richard's industriousness continued—and she had little doubt that it would—they could build a nest egg that might take them to Santa Barbara or Scottsdale or even Cancun. They could leave the farm behind, and she would never face filthy dishes stacked in stagnant sink water or endless menial chores or a firmament forever swaddled in gray. And surely Richard would never raise a hand against her. Not if she kept doing well. Not if she worked hard for him.

Headlights flashed against the front windows.

Theresa put down her still full, stone-cold cup of tea and sniffed the air one last time, testing it. The smell had mostly dissipated, and anyway, it didn't seem that bad now. She could get used to it.

She stood and went to let Collins in.

Coin-Op Carter
by Sean Benham

They were punishment for a lost bet one day, a curse from a bearded woman the next. The end result of a business venture gone sour, or sometimes it was a deal with the Devil. The edges of the smaller, vertical rectangle were tinged with a faint orange glow that burned from within. The larger, horizontal rectangle was a digital display; it didn't quite function like a cheap alarm clock, but it sure looked like one. You could have asked him about them a hundred times and you wouldn't have received the same answer twice. The truth was, he couldn't remember how he wound up with a coin-op slot and a countdown timer lodged in the middle of his chest.

His name was Carter, most likely. He didn't have any ID under that name, or any ID at all. What he did have was a jaggy, faded tattoo scrawled across his neck. It either read Carter or Carten, and he didn't respond kindly to Carten.

Carter was a bum if you appreciated the indelicate; he was perpetually down on his luck if you didn't. Slice the wording however you like, but one way or the other, he was homeless and used to be a fixture down on Main. He set up in front of the cake shop on weekdays, but when the weekend rolled around, a cupcake or two could usually convince him to relocate a ways down the block. The frame store didn't care for their unwelcome weekend guest, but they didn't have much to offer in exchange for him getting off of their stoop.

He was an odd sight, instantly recognizable. His hair did as it pleased, naturally tending to pile in a messy bird's nest on top of his head. He couldn't grow a proper beard, but that didn't stop him from trying. Long, graying scraggles jutted from his upper lip and drooped off of his chin. He was old, most likely. 55? 60? It was hard to say. He was pickled in hard living, indelicately preserved. Carter didn't dress for practicality or comfort. Winter or summer, rain or shine, he always wore the same crusty brown slacks and battered snow boots, opting to go without a shirt. He had to show off his moneymaker.

He was the only beggar on Main. The town wasn't overrun with the destitute, but it could sheepishly claim a handful. The rest of the panhandlers knew better than to veer onto Carter's turf; it just wasn't worth it. He wasn't violent, or even particularly mean. He was good at asking people for quarters, really good. And it had to be quarters; nickels and dimes wouldn't cut it. Pennies? He'd scoff if he liked you, gruffly tell you to piss off if he didn't. A dollar? Thanks, man, but go get it changed at the gas station.

He'd slowly tap the text on glowing coin slot and tell you what he was after, his voice slurred. "Quarters only." It actually read "Push to Reject," but after Carter's trademark spiel, no one felt inclined to correct him. His "sales pitch" was simple. He told passersby that life cost him a quarter an hour. The timer in his chest never had more than 59 minutes left on it.

No one wanted to feel responsible for a man's death over a piddling 25 cents, and the way Carter pleaded, he made sure they would feel responsible. His desperation was no act. He might not have had a clear understanding of how he landed in his predicament, but the consequences of going against the rules were crystal clear. If those quarters didn't keep coming, if the timer ever hit quadruple zero, that would be the end of Carter.

◆

It took Tara Millsap five and a half years to graduate from high school. She was in no rush. Over those 11 carefree semesters, she boasted a grade point average of 0.5 and an average blood alcohol content of 0.04. But she was never good with numbers. Or science. Or social studies, physical education, or English.

She was good at partying, though. Christ, she could throw 'em back. At her best, she'd put away two and a half six-packs in an afternoon before switching to gallon bottles of grocery store plonk in the evening. She did it all without spoiling her figure, as well. Hard to say whether or not it would catch up to her in time. She didn't live long enough to get fat.

♦

Carter liked to drink, too; that was no secret. He used to drink a lot more back when life wasn't metered at a quarter an hour. That is to say, he used to drink more alcohol, the "intended for human consumption" kind of alcohol. Carter still got sloppy drunk on a routine basis, but his cognac days were long over.

He started by shoplifting traditional near-liquor. No one was particularly appreciative that mouthwash eventually had to be removed from store shelves, stashed behind cash counters and made available only by respectable request. But a minor inconvenience to most was a challenge to Carter. He rose to the challenge by chugging hairspray, the kind that promised Maximum Hold also delivered maximum knocking-you-on-your-ass. Carter grew to become a big fan of Maximum Hold, or "Red Can," as he knew it.

Carter and Tara could have been drinking buddies, had things gone differently. They wouldn't have had much to talk about aside from their love of the drink, and he would've had at least 20 years on her, though stranger things have happened. But things didn't go differently and stranger things did happen.

♦

Tara joined the force the winter after graduation. Aside from making sure she didn't get busted for underage consumption or open container, Tara didn't have any particular interest in law and order during her time in school. But she had been fired from every taco joint and sub shop in town and needed to pay rent somehow. When she heard about how the police union ensured you couldn't get the axe no matter how badly you screwed up, she knew she had found her calling.

She lifted, ran, gripped, and swam well enough. She shot the center of mass six times out of ten. She guessed her way through the true and false. She drove the obstacle course without issue; she'd only had three and a half drinks that morning and chewed two sticks of gum to smell extra law-abiding. She signed some papers, then signed some more. She swore the oath with her toes crossed. She was in: Gun. Badge. Squad Car. Navy-blue uniform. Two-way radio. The prospect of an early retirement package. Some goddamn respect for once. It was all hers.

She was assigned to the southeast—far from downtown, one WASPy subdivision after another, sleepy as Hell. It didn't take Tara long to figure that being a cop was friggin' boring. But being a drunk cop? That was lots of fun. Vodka was her on-duty drink of choice; it mixed best with the coffee from Mackey's Diner. She kept a backup fifth in the glove box to keep the party going and she kept enough gum on hand to make sure she stayed spearminty.

Tara would routinely get sloppy and make the southeast her playground: driving too fast, shaking down the chop-suey house for free lunches, pulling guns to make a point. Work was a blurry blast, until Gonzalez got sick.

♦

Coin-Op Carter

Carter wasn't smart, but he was no dummy. He knew he had to play the pity game just right in order to keep the quarters coming. He always had more than 25 cents to his name, but it didn't pay to look that way. He let the meter run low, low enough to make it look as though death was never further than an hour away. The extra quarters were stashed in his back pocket, carefully wrapped in napkins to muffle the jingle.

When he was on the verge of passing out for the night, he'd wait until no one was looking, feed two bucks into his chest, and roll over, hiding the timer from whoever might pass as he slept. Carter may have had a bizarre technological affliction, but he'd managed it for years without issue. It got even easier once he switched from mouthwash to hairspray.

Bottles of mouthwash were meant to be opened and the contents were meant for your mouth. Neither of those statements could be made about cans of hairspray. Carter wasn't going to let the pictures of explosions and skulls on the cans of hairspray scare him, though. He was going to find a way into that aerosol fortress and get wasted on the chemical juice within. The first few tries started with a decent-sized rock poised to smash the can's nozzle. They ended with sticky, angry messes and a lot of wasted hairspray. Carter was forced to steal a better solution.

Peterson's Hardware didn't have any obvious security cameras and Carter didn't have much to lose, so he could afford to forego subtlety. The alley behind Peterson's wasn't well lit and the rear window wasn't latched. What was planned as a break and enter simply turned into an enter, and a leisurely one at that. Carter made a meal of impulse-buy beef jerky and left Peterson's with a hacksaw and a bag of shammy cloths.

He returned to the stoop of the cake store and celebrated with two Red Cans. The saw lopped the tops of the cans off quickly and cleanly, the rags saved the initial sticky burst of spray for later. Life was good, and it got even better once Carter realized he could cut more than spray cans.

He checked Peterson's, but they didn't have what he needed. The construction supply place down by the tracks was a fair bit farther than Carter usually liked to walk, but they had exactly what he was looking for. Even better, it was cheap—just about $6 per foot. He wasn't about to do the math, but he could see that if he did it right, he'd be buying far more than another six hours. He rummaged through his back pocket, placed a short night's sleep worth of change on the counter and walked out with a shiny steel rod, just under an inch in diameter.

It worked perfectly. The thin slugs he sawed off the end of the rod wouldn't pass for quarters in a store, but they were close enough to fool the meter.

Carter's life got a lot cheaper, allowing him to indulge in his favorite activity: drinking real liquor. He'd spent years chasing away the shakes with a class of booze far below consumer grade. It was only when he was finally able to switch back to rotgut whiskey that he remembered just how much he liked to drink.

In his mouthwash and hairspray days, the ultra high-proof liquor kept life tolerable, but the additives he was drinking along with it made him feel horrible. The bouts of dizzying diarrhea and fuzzy blind spots that lasted for hours went away after he made the leap back to real hooch, and he was actually buying what he drank. Yes, he was buying it with money he conned out of those who pitied him, but to Carter it was a moral victory, a cause for celebration. Celebration meant more drinking. A lot more.

Carter was a seasoned drinker, naturally, but once he was drinking for pleasure and not just chemical dependency, he started to overindulge. Missteps became staggers. Mutters grew into angry tirades. Crude comments once left unsaid were shouted at those who passed, often punctuated with wildly inappropriate gestures. With the timer no longer his primary concern, Carter turned from a harmless oddity into a damn good reason to cross the street.

The charitable quarter donations dropped off as Carter grew into an even greater lush. He'd still do pretty well in the mornings, before he had the chance to get good and lit, but after lunch, his drunken antics were enough to keep most of his prospective customers at bay. Carter didn't see any reason to cut back on his bad behavior; he was still pulling in more than enough for his daily rod and bottle. He didn't miss having to engage absolutely everyone that passed, if anything, it gave him time to think about old girlfriends, missed opportunities, and the ever-present threat of death housed in his chest.

He began to wonder if it really was counting down to the end, or if that was just a misguided notion brought about by a lifetime of letting ethanol scramble his wits. The phrase "maybe not ..." crept into his head from time to time, but he was always quick to silence it—sawing off another slug from the rod and buying himself yet another 60 minutes. Carter wouldn't take any chances.

♦

"A robbery suspect is fleeing westbound on—" *Yeah, boring.* "Goose in my cup, shorty like a truck, assmeat so fat, beepin' when she back it up ..." *Ooh, that's my jam!*

That was Tara's standard reply to a call for backup. Nobody told her what to do, so she treated radio dispatches as if they were advice from her stepmom. Let Gonzalez deal with the "hero cop" crap; she'd officer around on her own, thanks.

This call was different. It was going to suck. Hell, any call that she actually had to respond to sucked. Gonzalez was out sick, or so he claimed, which meant relying on the glory-hog white knight wasn't an option. And while the union made sure she'd never get canned, they didn't do a thing to keep the chief from bitching and moaning nonstop about "adequate levels of performance" and "being a piss-poor excuse for a cop." Tara had to do something to get on his good side; the last time she was called into his office, he flashed some official-looking papers and talked a big game about "busting her butt down to janitor unless she showed some immediate improvement." It was either deal with this call or trade in her gun for a toilet brush.

"This is Millsap, car 6-1-6. I'm on it."

Some bum had broken a window down on Main. Shouldn't have been a big deal, but he was making it a big deal by waving a goddamn saw around. Great.

A quick pit stop behind the tire store, five strong belts of hero juice and two sticks of gum later, Tara was as ready as she was going to get. She had slept through the "Levels of Crazy" slideshow during her training, so she wasn't sure what to expect or even how to act in a situation like this. She would let her liquor-borne courage and state-issued sidearm take the lead.

Tara took her time driving down to Main, mostly due to her indifferent attitude to police work, partly because she got lost. She never went downtown, even off-duty. The place was a dump, full of low-life weirdos like this guy. She didn't know why he had decided to tape clock-radio parts to himself or why anybody bothered to call the cops if all he was doing was sitting on the curb and crying. She didn't care much, either. She was there, he was there, he had a saw on his lap, she was a cop. This could only go one way.

"Drop it! Put the saw on the ground, now!"

"I'm sorry!" Carter howled in between sniffles, his eyes red and watery.

"I said drop it, asshole!" Tara cocked the hammer of her service revolver. Nothing felt quite as good as pairing a pointed gun with a menacing sound. The bum let the saw fall to the ground, of course.

"I said I'm sorry! I tripped! I tripped and I-I dropped the metal stick in the drain. I didn't mean to, I swear! And I'm outta quarters! Look! Look at it!"

He pointed frantically to the clock on his chest: 00:04.

"Yeah, nice clock. Now get on the ground and spread 'em!"

"Give me a quarter. Can you give me a quarter? Please, I don't have much time left!"

"I said press your nasty gut to the ground before I blast it, dickhead."

Weeping, Carter collapsed to the pavement with a thud. Tara pounced, landing on his back, knees first. Cuffs were applied, admonitions shouted.

"You think these nice people like having their place smashed up, you stupid son of a bitch?"

"I didn't mean to! I fell and the window was in my way! And then I dropped the metal stick, and … gimme a quarter! Please!"

"Shut up and stand up."

Tara nearly fell over backward as she tugged the grimy bastard to his feet. Making an officer look awkward couldn't go without punishment. With a flick of her wrist, Tara spun the revolver on her palm. With a twist of her hips, she smashed the bum's nose with the butt of her gun.

"Stop resisting!"

The stream of tears pouring down Carter's face diluted the blood dripping from his nose. He sputtered and spat as Officer Millsap shoved him toward the rear seat of the cruiser.

"I need to feed the meter! I will die if I don't feed the meter!"

"Aw, poor ugly baby let his meter go hungry?" Tara leaned in close to taunt Carter. She instantly regretted pulling the green blob of gum from her mouth; his natural stink stung her nostrils once she was without the minty vapor barrier. Even more reason to put him in his place. "Open wide, you sack of shit." Her face scowled into an odor-averse wince, she smeared the gum along the length of the coin-op slot. Touching this guy any more than she had to was gross, but the look of sheer terror on his face was well worth it.

Carter thrashed and squirmed, the cuffs cutting into his leathery wrists. He began to wail. If the throaty forlorn cries spewing out of him were supposed to be words, they sure as Hell weren't in English. It was annoying, but his awful commotion let Tara know that she'd won. This bum would think twice before he decided to disrupt an officer of the law's aimless driving around again.

Shoving him into the backseat wasn't easy. He was heavier than he looked and wouldn't stop convulsing. At least she wouldn't have to pry him back out again; she'd leave that to the boys at the drunk tank. She pulled away from the scene of the "crime" and roared onto the freeway, making a beeline back to the station uptown with the siren blaring. Tara couldn't wait to get Carter out of her cruiser; his non-stop noisemaking was really getting old.

Traffic on the freeway was light and eagerly accommodated the screaming siren and spinning lights. Tara had the two leftmost lanes to herself. She straddled the dashed white line, pedal pushed low. Even over the din of the siren, she could hear Carter come to his senses. The bum had finally shut up.

She turned to gloat, looking to twist the knife a little, to stomp her victory home. Carter's twitching had stopped. The timer on his chest was blinking in time with the siren: 00:00. 00:00. 00:00. Tara couldn't be certain, but it looked like Carter's breathing had stopped, too.

"Oh, goddamn it! This is the last thing I—"

She gagged and retched as the smell filled the cruiser, and flinched as the seam of his pants tore wide.

♦

Officer Gonzalez was on break—whiling away the time in Mackey's diner, chugging down coffee and making friendly shop-talk with Officer Trent. Trent was green, but his story was wild. Bachelor party gone wrong, strippers in the ER, two little dogs rolling around in cocaine …

Gonzalez had to cut Trent short. As the senior officer, it was his unwritten duty to keep the rookie from trumping him at storytime.

"Man, that's nothing. I mean, it's not nothing, but listen: you ever work with Officer Millsap? You around back then?"

Trent shook his head as he took a short sip of coffee, trying to hide his disappointment in being cut off.

"No, didn't know him. I don't think."

"Her. And you'd remember her, trust me. Tits out to here, couldn't get her vest closed all the way. Wasn't cut out for the job, though. I've seen some bad cops come and go, but she was the worst. Bad attitude, worse people skills. You know why she's not on the force anymore?"

"No, why?"

"She's dead. Died in the line of duty."

"Damn."

"Yeah. She's not on the fallen plaque back at the station, though. 'Cause of the way she died."

"It's that bad? What happened?"

"It was weird. The chief doesn't like to talk about it, thinks it makes the force look bad. So if this ever comes up, you didn't hear it from me, okay?"

"Yeah, of course."

"Good. She crashed her cruiser, wrapped the thing around a lamp post on Highway 5." Gonzalez paused for effect. It worked; Trent didn't look wowed in the least.

"That's it?"

"Nope, not even close. I said it was weird, right? So, they find the car on the side of the road but they can't see inside. Like, they can see something in there, but they don't know what it is. Something big, it looks like. Whatever it is, they can't see Millsap through it. Can't see anything through it.

So, the jaws of life come out, they get started on the door and

FWOOSH! Shit-covered quarters spill all over the road. And not just a few, either. I mean, the cruiser was full to the ceiling with shitty change. Had to call in the hazmat crew to clean things up."

An incredulous smile crept across Trent's face. "Shit-covered quarters? Right. Good one, Gonzo."

"No joke, man. Hand to God, that's how it went down. You're good to get these coffees? I've gotta hit the john."

I Dated Mother Nature

by Joshua Harding

I guess the ex I remember most is Mother Nature—or Gaia, as she prefers to be called. What more could a man want, really? She was fertility incarnate, a living Venus of Willendorf, a walking, talking cornucopia of procreation. Her hips were rolling hillocks, alive with the sound of music. Her auburn hair would whisk against her smooth shoulders with the hush of a Montana wheat field.

She was a jealous bitch, though. She'd flood my apartment with heavy rains or drop a tree in front of me if I so much as looked at another woman. Our relationship was, to use a cliché, a little stormy at times. But God, did she have great tits!

My older sister had dragged me to a party in the Jersey suburbs so I could meet some people and maybe find a job and maybe become more responsible. I'd just graduated from Colgate in the class of '58 with a degree in literature (or "filth," according to my mother), and I realized the moment the hostess took my coat that I didn't fit in and never would. I was an artist—a poet—with a spine-cracked copy of *A Coney Island of the Mind* in my pocket. I had nothing in common with those workaday types. You could practically scrape their quiet desperation off the floor.

I happened to notice a book strategically placed on the coffee table: Henry Miller's *Under the Roofs of Paris*. Its title peeked out furtively from beneath the latest issue of *Woman's Day*. The hostess, a childless suburban housewife and high school friend of my sister's, was trying very hard to advertise that she was into banned books. Too bad no one at the party (including her) had actually read the thing and knew the saucy nuances contained inside.

I looked at the book and then at the room full of people all wearing their Chanel and Dior with the sable fur trim, and thought: *These ladies think of themselves as worldly and scandalous. They wish they were having affairs (with Henry Miller in Paris) while their husbands are out playing golf. They need to get out more.* And I wondered how many of the husbands were doing just that to their wives—screwing someone at the office or the trade show or the regional sales meeting.

You'd think it would be so sordid and shocking that they're having these affairs, but it's really just boring. Poems, stories, or films dealing with these interpersonal matters have never held my interest. I've had enough relationship drama in my own life; I don't need to get more of it from my art. I'd rather read or write a piece that makes you think, makes you wonder, makes you say, "I've never read anything like that before!" Throw some robots or zombies in there.

It occurred to me that these suburban housewives and husbands were robots and zombies in their own right, going through their boring lives with their boring affairs at their boring party. And I realized I'd listened three times to the same story from this guy in a sweater vest about an ordeal of a hailstorm and his insurance company and his vinyl siding. I was ready to unzip my pants and start masturbating on the carpet just to change the subject when she whispered in my ear, "You got a cigarette?"

I guess next time around I'd like a real woman as opposed to a goddess. A woman who might not care that I once dated someone else years before I ever met her. It got to the point that if Gaia and I were walking somewhere and I happened to cast a sideways glance across the street, she'd think I was ogling another woman. Perhaps I would see a convenience store getting robbed or a circus elephant selling drugs to kids or a double-parked flying saucer.

Gaia would screech at me: "Who's that!?"

"No one," I'd respond.

I Dated Mother Nature

"Tell me who's over there!"

"No one!" I'd insist.

"Who are you fucking over there?!"

After we split up, I started to notice a lot of weird things. Dogs would growl and cats would spit and scratch at me as I passed. Not just my friends' pets or strays, but puppies and kittens in pet stores. Birds would dive bomb my head. Raccoons and skunks and squirrels leapt out at me from garbage cans and telephone poles. Going to the zoo was out of the question. One day, it hailed in a torrent, but only on the spot where my car was parked. When the squall was over, all that was left was a pockmarked hulk surround by a pool of shattered glass and ice.

Here's something to keep you up at night: Mother Nature is on a constant quest to kill you. From the moment you're born, she's got your number. We all have expiration dates, like eggs or cartons of milk. She'll try and take you out with diseases, parasites, genetic anomalies, tornadoes, earthquakes, shark attacks. Even with foot fungus and jock itch, it's like she's trying to decompose you while you're still alive.

Inevitably, she will kill everything and everyone. She must reap what she sows.

Mother Nature isn't the benevolent, matronly earth goddess we've all come to know—she's the Hindu Kali: a Darwinian, naturally selective creator and destroyer of billions.

What struck me first were her eyes: one blue and one brown, like a husky's. And she was dressed, well, unusually for cocktail party. A loose pyramid dress in a loud paisley pattern clung to her breasts and hips with an anxious quiver. She wore enormous bronze hoop earrings shrouded by the mahogany waterfall of her hair. Shiny bangles flashed at her wrists and a long strand of beads with tiny birds and flowers hung about her ivory throat. She was petite and curvaceous, unlike the rigid sticks of the other women at the party. Her legs were strong and muscular and, I noticed with a start, weren't shaved. She was also barefoot.

Her lips—miniature, rose-colored pillows—parted slowly again. "I said, 'You got a cigarette?'"

I was mute. I fumbled in my coat and produced a rumpled pack I'd been nursing for a few days and offered her one.

"Thanks," she said. "Join me outside for a smoke?"

I looked around the living room, where at least eight other people were puffing away. The hostess waved a Virginia Slim at the end of a long, black holder and her husband chewed on a briar pipe, trying desperately to look the part of the wizened lord of the manor. Besides, it was mid-May; the trees were still naked and the high earlier in the day hadn't been much above 50 degrees.

"Outside?" I asked.

"Yeah," she replied with a smile. Her teeth flashed a brilliant white, and her canines were slightly longer than the surrounding incisors. "Why not?"

In the backyard, she sat down on a clump of moss just within the bower of the forest that bordered the subdivision. "Mmm, Sphagnum flexuosum," she said as she wriggled her butt into the green carpet. She patted the ground for me to join her.

"Are you a botanist?" I asked. Gingerly, I lowered my ass down to the ground beside her knowing I'd look like I'd shit myself later and would need to visit the dry cleaner. The moss was cushiony and soft but also damp and freezing.

"Yes, and a zoologist, and an ornithologist, ichthyologist, and geologist—you name it."

"You're teasing," I replied. I realized I hadn't introduced myself and reached out my hand as the moisture soaked my trousers. "I'm Aaron. Aaron Sutherland."

"And I'm Mother Nature," she said, shaking my hand. Her palms were rough like a kitten's tongue and her grip was as firm as a cowboy's. "But you can call me Gaia."

Then she kissed me.

Before I could object, she'd mashed her lips against mine hungrily. I had a lungful of smoke I hadn't exhaled. Her tongue wormed its way between my lips and teeth, and she sucked the smoke out of my throat. Her arms were around my neck and her right leg swung over my hips. She released the kiss and let me get some air while she fixed me with her malamute eyes.

She smelled great—not flowery or powdery with dashes of French perfume, but musky and sweaty, full of pheromones and promise. She flipped a main circuit in me unlike any coed ever had back at Colgate. She grasped at my belt and started undoing my trousers.

"Are we crazy?!" I whispered.

It was the best I ever had.

She made me feel like Adonis, like I had the body of a Greek god and my erect cock was a lightning rod through which all good things were possible. Her body moved with my body like a symphony: first adagio and slow, then allegro and rapid. It was every metaphor in the universe: earth-shattering, toe-curling, angel-weeping. I felt like I could do anything or be anything in the world. I looked up and noticed leaves on the trees above us that weren't there before.

"What did you say your name was?" I asked when we were done.

"I told you," she said, sliding off my hips, "I'm Gaia. I'm also Isis, Ishtar, Mama Pacha, and Ibu Pertiwi. I'm Mother Nature."

I guess I was feeling gregarious and cocksure and elated at the time. Completely high on post-coital bliss, I probably would've believed anything.

Just then, a doe glided from out of the bushes nearby. She was completely silent. Her ear flicked as Gaia held out her hand. The deer stepped toward us so close I could see the coin-slot pupils of her chocolate-colored eyes. She nuzzled Gaia's hand and folded her slender legs and knelt down beside us.

"Hello, Odocoileus virginianus," she said. I'd never seen one so close before, only dead at the side of the highway or mounted above a fireplace. Then she laid her velvet head in my lap.

I no longer felt cold. Fireflies illuminated the air around us. Squirrels gathered in the branches. An owl hooted somewhere in the forest. It was like a scene from a cartoon where the young princess cleans the house or gets ready for the ball with all the little animals as her attendants. They gathered close to us and nestled in the moss as if they were stable animals kneeling before a holy crèche.

Gaia twirled her fingers above the ground and a dozen wildflowers sprouted before my eyes. They shook and elongated like a time-lapse film until the whole bower was blooming and lush.

The back door of the house creaked open and my sister poked her head out.

"Aaron?" she called. "Aaron, where've you gone? I have someone I want you to meet." Gaia grasped my hand and we scampered off into the forest like Adam and Eve escaping the searching eyes of God.

Back at my apartment in Soho, we fucked until sometime after four in the morning. My cat watched us patiently from the fire escape. Again and again, we locked together in our sacred love ritual. When I finally lost count, I collapsed onto my pillow, exhausted.

"What's the matter?" Gaia asked from the dark next to me. "Can't keep up?"

I was asleep before I could answer.

In the morning, I found her staring out the window at the street six floors below. She seemed distant and withdrawn. I kissed her hair.

"Morning. You tired?" I asked.

"No," she replied. "Just … too citified. Domesticated." I followed her gaze to the one tree on the sidewalk. It was stunted and stretched feebly from the concrete where it was rooted up to the few shafts of pale sunlight that broke over the canyon walls of the buildings.

"Let's go get breakfast." I said. "I'm starving."

Gaia brightened. "Me too!" she smiled. "And after, let's go to Central Park."

We went to a diner on Sixth Avenue. I had coffee and a croissant; she had steak and eggs.

"What about unicorns?" I asked.

"What?" she said, licking steak sauce from her fingers.

"Unicorns. You told me what happened to the dinosaurs. What happened to the unicorns?"

"I had to get rid of them because they were always poking each other's eyes out." She tore a bit of gristle off the bone and winked at me.

"Well then, what about mermaids?" I sipped my coffee and glanced across the street.

"Never you mind about them," she replied.

On the opposite sidewalk, an old man shambled by with a newspaper tucked under his arm. He was wearing a VFW cap studded with pins.

"What are you looking at?" Gaia asked. There was more interrogation in her voice than I liked.

"Just an old veteran on the sidewalk," I replied. She followed my gaze to the old man. While she stared, he suddenly clutched at his left arm. He staggered and braced himself on a tenement's stair rail. I looked back at Gaia. Her eyes seemed to widen like a cat's do when it's stalking prey. The old man crumpled to the sidewalk. His newspaper fluttered away down the street as a passing sailor and his date scurried to his side and waved for help.

"Did … did you just do that?" I asked, losing my appetite.

"Of course I did." She picked at her teeth with a fork. "I had to make room."

"Make room? That's rather cold-hearted!"

She fixed me with her bicolor eyes. "Are you kidding? I just created a baby in the couple at the next table. They made love this morning and I just made them conceive. That's what I do: make love and make room."

We took the subway from Bleeker Street to Lexington and 63rd. She seemed to know everyone—ticket takers, conductors, street musicians, bums with their hats out—it was like old home days at every stop. We hopped of at Grand Central so I could buy more cigarettes, and she spotted a scrawny Puerto Rican who was playing a tenor sax and sitting on a metal bucket. Gaia greeted him with a double-breasted embrace.

"Tito!" she cried as if seeing a long-lost loved one. The man rose and allowed her to fold him into her arms. He was short and scraggy. A weed patch of stubble peppered his mocha-colored chin. He was wearing a porkpie hat and a three-piece suit that was too big for him and shiny with filth. I thought I smelled urine.

They chatted about his music and his kids while I stood aside and tried to look interested in an ad for mouthwash. When they were done, Tito nodded toward his saxophone's case where a few coins and rumpled bills lay about. Gaia reached into her coat and withdrew not money, but a bottle of cabernet and an ounce of marijuana.

Inside the park, Gaia headed straight for the Ramble. The sounds of the city muffled and died away as we entered the enclosing trees and bushes. The gray branches were just starting to bud and birds flitted about on the slender branches. Squirrels chirruped as we passed.

"Hello, Sciurus carolinensis!" Gaia said, then she stripped naked faster than Tarzan returning to Africa.

"Hey!" I hissed. "You're going to get arrested." I looked over my shoulder down the path from where we'd come.

"And what's so bad about that?" she asked.

"I don't have bail money for you."

"Relax. You need to get out more."

I immediately spotted another couple, both men. They hadn't

noticed us. Gaia approached them with no regard for her nakedness.

"Ted! Gary!" she called. The men turned with a start and dread in their eyes. Their fear melted when they saw her.

"Oh, it's you, Gaia," said the first. He was tall and dark-haired and wore a black turtleneck under his tweed. I noticed the other—a shorter man with curly blond hair—was surreptitiously buttoning his trousers. "I almost didn't recognize you."

"How've you two been?" Gaia asked. She kissed each one on the cheek.

"Didn't recognize her, Ted?" asked the second. "If she'd had clothes on, then I could understand not recognizing her. How've you been, love?"

The three caught up on Ted's work at the firm and Gary's ailing mother. As they chatted, I noticed the two men were holding hands.

"Oh, I almost forgot," said Gaia all at once, "Ted, Gary, this is Aaron."

The two men shook my hand warmly. "Pleased to meet you," they said in unison.

"Likewise," I replied, withdrawing my hand.

After Ted and Gary left, I turned to Gaia. "How can you be so familiar with them?"

"What?" she asked.

"You call yourself Mother Nature and what they're doing is so … unnatural."

Gaia responded with a frown, "Don't tell me what's unnatural. Love is natural. Affection is natural. It doesn't matter what goes where." She grabbed my tie and pulled me closer to her satin skin (God, was she beautiful!). I could feel myself straining at my zipper. "The fact that you're still wearing that button-down straightjacket while I'm here, in front of you, naked and all-access—that's unnatural!"

A week later, I took her to a poetry reading down in Greenwich.

The club was deep within the tenement canyons of Sullivan and Houston, not a blade of grass or leaf or tree to be seen for blocks. Gaia was already in a sour mood when we arrived. The place was crowded and nicotine-fogged. There were goatees and black turtlenecks everywhere you looked. A sax played plaintively and forlornly from a corner.

My poem was third in the lineup.

I took the stage and grasped the microphone, releasing a squeal of feedback. A sea of sunglasses turned toward me and the sax player paused, waiting to hear the tempo of my piece so he could match it. I took a deep breath and read:

> If death
> were perhaps a woman
> forged of cold ice
> and iron deception
> I would deceive her
> kiss her cold lips
> My lips would stick
> for just a second
> as I betrayed her

The crowd erupted in a snapping of fingers and the sax finished with a honking flourish as I stepped down, elated.

I saw Gaia and knew immediately there would be consequences.

"What'd you think?" I asked as I kissed her cheek.

"That was about me, wasn't it?" Her arms were crossed over her enormous breasts.

"No," I replied. "I wrote that ages ago."

She blew a lock of hair away from her brow and squinted her husky eyes at me. "Well, I won't criticize the poem ... or the poet. Nothing is as sacred as creation, no matter who your muse might be."

I Dated Mother Nature

"Aaron!"

I turned and found Tina Mitchell, an old girlfriend from high school, making her way toward us through the crowd. She was brunette and ivory-skinned and wore a frock coat and silk scarf—a sophisticated princess among the bohemian crowd. As she drew near, she clasped my hand and kissed me on the cheek.

"That was a beautiful piece, Aaron," she said. "How have you been?"

"Wonderful," I said. "How is Smith these days?"

"Dreadful." She turned to Gaia, "Hello, I'm Tina. Aaron and I are old friends." She reached out a slender hand to shake hands.

Gaia was as frigid as the poem made her out to be, but at least she returned the gesture.

"So sorry," I said. "Tina, this is Gaia; we met through my sister. Tina and I went to high school together, Gaia."

"Don't let his dark poetry fool you, Gaia. Underneath Aaron's brooding exterior lies a true gentleman."

"Oh, really?" asked Gaia turning to me. I noticed she held onto Tina's hand for a moment longer than normal.

"Oh, yes," said Tina finally withdrawing her hand from Gaia's grasp. "He's been known to rescue kittens from trees." Someone called Tina's name from across the room. "Well, I must be off. Take care of yourself, Aaron. Gaia, very nice to meet you."

"The same," said Gaia. She smiled, but there was no joy in it.

Tina squeezed back through the crowd and over to a knot of friends.

"You still have feelings for her, don't you?" Gaia asked. I could feel a chill on my neck as she uttered the question.

"No," I said. "But I don't have any ill will toward her."

"You're still sleeping with her, aren't you?"

I was completely flummoxed. "How could I?" I asked, sounding more defensive than I would've liked. "I've been with you every moment for the past week." Gaia followed Tina's retreating back through the crowd. Her eyes widened and her pupils dilated until they looked like onyx pennies.

I grasped her forearm. "You're not going to kill her, are you?"

She turned to me. From her eyes I gaped the depths of the deepest ocean, the darkest fissure in the earth. "No," she responded, "not now. Cervical cancer will get her in ten years." I looked at her, horrified. "Oh, don't worry," she said, taking my hand. "She'll have two kids before then. Her genes will make it into the next generation."

We lasted until the height of summer. The trees were lush and full in their emerald beauty. We kept the windows open around the clock and let the breezes cool our bodies in the steaming afternoons and velvet nights. Gaia seemed to come into a heavy presence as if the fruitfulness of the season resonated in her every pore.

We were in New Jersey at my sister's place. She and her husband were in Connecticut on a friend's boat, so we had the house to ourselves. We lounged in the backyard, smoking, drinking Riesling, and sunbathing. Next door, a little boy—no more than six or seven—swam in a large, turquoise pool. He splashed and giggled and wore a giant, white Styrofoam egg strapped around his chest. From the house, I heard his mother say, "Peter, I have to make a phone call. You stay in the shallow end."

The screen door slammed and the little boy continued to splash about.

Gaia finished her wine with a gulp, took a deep drag on her cigarette, and looked toward the side of the house. I thought she was watching a buzzard wheel over the freeway to the west when I saw her bicolored eyes widen just like they did with the old man outside the diner. Her pupils spread inky and wide like camera shutters and I realized I hadn't heard the kid splash for several moments.

I shot up in my lawn chair and craned my neck over the fence. He was facedown in the water. The Styrofoam float had slid down to his waist, raising his hips and pushing his head deeper under the surface. He wasn't moving. I dropped my cigarette, vaulted the fence and plunged into the pool.

In my arms, the boy seemed so small and limp. I hauled him onto the pool deck as all my Boy Scout First Aid training flooded back into my brain. I was slapping his back as he coughed and wheezed and his mother came flying out of the screen door toward us.

Gaia was furious. "What do you think you're doing?" she shrieked at me when I came back into my sister's yard. "You're messing with the balance!"

"What?" I snapped back, "The balance of making room? Look, Gaia, it's one thing when it's a hawk eating a mouse or a deer struck down by a car, or even an old man who's lived a long life. But this is a kid!"

"You wouldn't get between a cougar and her prey, would you?"

"Looks as if I just did."

"Maybe I should just take you in the boy's place."

"Gaia," I said, toweling myself off roughly, "We're through." She looked at me, perplexed, as if no one had ever uttered these words to her before. "I'm catching a cab back to the city. You can find your own way home to wherever you live." (We'd never spent a night at her place, come to think of it.) "Hitch a ride from some random stranger; you seem to know them all."

I've been single for almost six weeks now. Well, as single as anyone can be with Mother Nature surrounding him every day and every night.

I don't miss her. Don't get me wrong, the sex was great—if I'm never with another woman for the rest of my days, I'll be all right—but I don't miss her. I miss my cat. I found her when I got back to Manhattan after that fateful day. She'd been run over by a taxi outside of my apartment.

Single is fine, though. I'm writing more poetry and getting stuff done around the apartment. I've found I'm most at peace in the places where nothing natural can get in: elevators, parking garages, walk-in freezers. I don't eat at restaurants much anymore, though, not since that Chinese place where my fortune cookie told me to watch my back.

Seeing my parents in Connecticut has been problematic, too. Sophie, their Cavalier King Charles spaniel, flies into a rage and goes for my throat each time I visit. I haven't seen my sister in over a month, either. She'd complained she was tired the last I'd spoken with her on the phone. Heart disease runs in our family, so I started grilling her about shortness of breath, chest pains, numbness or weakness in her arms.

"When did you become such a medico?" she asked.

"No reason," I said as I thumbed through a copy of *Folk Medicine.* "Can't a guy worry about his sister's health?" I pulled the surgical mask tighter over my ears.

"You're sweet, but it's nothing," she said.

I changed the subject. "I heard the weather forecast for tonight; supposed to be thunderstorms. Make sure you stay clear of the windows and unplug the television."

"Aaron, are you all right?"

"I'm fine," I replied.

"Well, take care of yourself and don't be such a shut-in. You need to get out more."

I do take care of myself, I thought as we said our goodbyes. *I'll take care of me and you, and mom and dad—everyone. I have to. I have to, knowing my ex is out there, somewhere, waiting to kill us all.*

Annunciation

by Alicia Cusano-Weissenbach

You ain't supposed to see stuff like that, so you just pretend you don't. It ain't so weird, y'know. There's lots of stuff like that— normal stuff that you ain't supposed to see—so you just keep walking.

Y'know what I mean, don't you? Like when some fat bitch smacks her kid upside the face in a store and you feel bad, 'cause y'know, you been that kid. Or when you're walking home and you see some guy tweaking, and it's the middle of the day and he's on the sidewalk in front of his building, but you just keep walking.

This is like that, but it ain't. Difference is that other people see them things and y'know it 'cause they're trying so hard *not* to, but with this, no one but me and Benny see it. I saw it first, and then Benny did, but not 'til I pointed and made him look at it.

Well, actually, that ain't entirely true, 'cause y'see, I think my intestines felt it first. They sorta clenched up and got all wiggly-feeling, like they was bursting, and that's how I knew to look.

Benny says it's probably 'cause I got a worm, like the one we saw at the Mütter Museum when his parents took us to Philly. That place was all full of messed-up shit, like body parts in jars and the original Siamese twins. Wish I could be stuck on Benny like that. Guess you'd get tired of being together like that after a while, though.

Still, I had to show Benny, 'cause nothing impresses him. He's too smart for school, and he gets A's even though he cuts class. He comes down to see me 'cause it really ain't that far away from where his parents live. They're the richest people I ever saw, and they live in the good part of the borough. We don't go there 'cause people stare at us.

People here stare at Benny, too, but no one ever tried to jump him. He's asthmatic and thin, and he's got skin like cream. Wears a Rolex at age 14 and has his little suit like a little business person 'cause his school makes him wear it—and he walks down the street alone!

"You," he'd said, pointing at me one day. I was reading *The Outsiders* and thinking how I wished our gangs was like them. I looked at him and thought I was seeing Gabriel. "I want you to come with me."

I was ten, and he picked me, just like that. Ever since then, we been together. I ain't never been able to repay him 'til I thought of this.

I was breathing real fast. I was so excited that I was holding his hand and pulling him along, even though I know he hates that. He don't like being touched, but when I showed him, he stopped acting pissed off. He close to shit himself.

I mean, there's a fuckin' plant growing up out of the middle of the street and into the clouds. I always seen it, but the one time I pointed it out, Mamma slapped me right in my face and 'bout broke my nose.

"Liars go to Hell, you understand, Annunziata Bianca? Do I need to warsh out your mouth with soap?"

"But I *saw* it!" I insisted, spitting 'cause I could already taste the orange Dial.

"Do you want me to tell Papi?"

I shook my head real hard, 'cause Papi hits with his fist. 'Least Mamma and Nonna keep their hands open. Nonna was there too, and she grabbed me by the hair and drug me into my room where the biggest Jesus in the house is, with all the paint on His face chipped off so I used to get nightmares from it and cry 'cause it looks like someone jumped Him and fucked Him up good, maybe with acid. Nonna won't throw that thing away, 'cause she brought it from Rome, and it's the most important thing she got—that's why it gets to hang next to her framed picture of Il Duce.

And she drug me in front of that Jesus and Mussolini and told me to pray and save my soul from the Devil and never to lie again. She warshed out my mouth with the Dial after, just to make sure, though. *Blah.*

Benny's parents ain't like that. They wouldn't believe in the plant neither, but they ain't like that.

When he saw it, all growing up out of the pavement like a ladder into Heaven, he told me we couldn't tell no one. He was shocked, and I was proud of that. Usually he just smiles at me when I try to surprise him or make him laugh.

"We could tell your mom and your dad," I suggested. I knew they wouldn't believe it, but it was funny to think what they'd say.

My brother Angelo likes to say rich people are crazy. Instead of slapping you in your goddamn lying mouth, they smile, indulgent-like, and tell you what a good imagination you got, and maybe you should write it down in a journal. And they don't drag you off to church and throw your ass in the hot box to confess, 'cause they want you to "have freedom to find your own spirituality." Crazy, like I said.

I thought Kafka's parents was like that, 'cause he was so creative, but Benny laughed at me for saying that, and said Kafka's dad was actually a piece of shit. 'Course he never said "piece of shit," 'cause Benny don't ever cuss.

Thought for sure he'd cuss when he saw the plant, but he just walked all the way 'round, careful in that way he always is, looking at it intently, frowning. After a while of staring, he touched it, one finger, then two, then his whole palm.

I was waiting with bated breath like them girls in adventure novels do when their knight's gonna kiss 'em. Benny tells me not to read that shit, so usually I stick to "good" stuff like Shakespeare. He's okay once you learn how to read him, but when I found out he ripped off a bunch of dead Greek guys, I was kinda pissed.

"It's real," Benny said, all surprised. He's got this lock of hair, all dark and shiny, that falls over his beautiful white forehead sometimes, and I noticed it was doing that. He was too distracted to move it, though. I wanted to move it for him, and I almost reached out.

"Yeah," I said, stupid and happy.

He looked at me, and I got a thrilling chill right down to my belly. His eyes are blue, cool and frosty like a bottle of fancy vodka.

"How long have you known about this?"

"Oh, forever!" My chest 'bout swelled up big as a robin's. "Been here since I was four. Just showed up one day."

"Annie, only you could keep a giant beanstalk to yourself for nine years."

The way he said it sorta made me feel bad. He didn't need to ask why he couldn't see it before and I could, or why a red Schwinn rode right through it, and the guys 'bout to steal the Schwinn walked through right after and passed by us.

Things are always that way. People don't see things they don't want to, even when they're right there, obvious to me. Benny wants to see things clear, but he only sees people clear. Think that's why he picked me, 'cause he was seeing that I was seeing. I didn't tell him 'bout the plant before 'cause I was used to seeing it, and only thought of it on a whim 'cause he was bored.

"So what you wanna do?"

"It requires thought, don't you think? I'm going to sleep on it. You hungry?"

Annunciation

I was, so he took me back to his fancy apartment. They call it their "flat" even though that word don't make a lot of sense. British, they said. He used to take me places to eat, but when his parents found out he was doing it to avoid seeing them, they took his credit card. Fuckin' 14-year-old with a credit card, can you believe it?

Already told you that his parents are crazy. I could tell Benny was hoping they was still out, but they came in and was all smiles. I want to be like them someday—they don't do work, they just write shit all day about plays and paintings and crap, and they get paid.

Don't make no sense. Mamma sews at her alteration shop 'til that space under her nails is bleeding, and Nonna's fingers is all knotted up so they look like two big potatoes from doing the same thing. Papi hauls stuff for the city. That's work, and ain't no one ever got paid for doing work.

"Annunziata, sweetheart!" His mom was always calling me "Annunziata" instead of "Annie," 'cause she thought I should be proud of my "ethnic identity." Like that one Christmas Eve when she cooked all them fishes and spaghetti that wasn't like no spaghetti Nonna ever made, saying it was so I could celebrate *La Vigilia*. I said we don't do that and we eat ham, and she 'bout cried, so I lied and said I was joking. Then I choked down two plates of her shitty homemade spaghetti and Benny laughed at me later when I was throwing it up.

"Hi, Mrs. Engel."

"How are you, Annunziata?" Benny's dad asked. He squeezed my shoulder but he didn't touch Benny. Like I said, Benny don't like being touched.

They was 40-something, wearing silk like they was going out somewhere even though they was probably staying in, and Mrs. Engel had skin like a 20-year-old. Mr. Engel was blond and pale, and I guess pretty normal.

"I'm fine, thank you. Is it okay to stop by?" It's almost another language when you're speaking to them, like Italian or Shakespeare or whatever. They look all worried when I start to talk like I do with my brothers, so I talk the way they want. Makes 'em feel like they helped me or something. Benny don't care how I say things, just what I say. Makes it hard to bullshit him.

"It's always okay!" Mrs. Engel told me. She gave me a hug. Her perfume smelled real good, and if I'm ever rich like her, I want to smell like that. She picked a thread off of my shirt and pressed her lips together. "You certainly are rough on your clothes. When I was out shopping today, though, I found you some really cute skirts and blouses. I hope you don't mind!"

I looked at Benny, and his eyes was frostier than normal. "*Mom*," he said in a low voice.

"Oh, she doesn't mind, does she?"

"Thank you," I mumbled. She likes buying me clothes, but I always gotta rip the labels out and scuff 'em up. Ain't no one gonna jump Benny, but *me*—they'd cut up my face and steal my shoes like they done to Sheena Watkins if they thought I was acting better than I am.

"Are you staying for dinner, dear?" Mrs. Engel asked. Mr. Engel didn't say nothing; Benny says he learned not to say nothing around women a long time ago. He got real good at smiling.

"We *just* came for a snack, *Mother*." Benny was staring 'em down, and if I ever looked at my parents that way, they'd lock me in a closet.

"Well, there's cake in the kitchen if you want."

"Yes, thanks, *Susan*."

"Anything going on?" Mrs. Engel was smiling at Benny, looking like a desperate junkie, just waiting for him to say, "Yeah, I've got the dope." And she wanted him to give her something so bad, and you could see it, like she was wanting to get baked bad on what he had, but he was saying, "No deal, keep your money. I already made bank off of some eighth grader."

I looked at my beat-up Reeboks, feeling that kinda hot-box shame 'til his parents was gone.

When they was, I looked at Benny again, and all I could think was how that space between his dark eyebrows was furrowed.

◆

After that, we talked about the plant every day. Benny would ask me to take him to it, and he'd walk all 'round it and take notes and make little pictures that he'd only show me half of. I knew what he was planning, but I never said. I didn't think it was a good idea, 'cause it made my guts clench up. But I liked watching him concentrate and look at the plant with his frosted eyes.

One day, we was at it all afternoon, then we went to my house to get some water.

My brother Lorenzo was sitting on the couch doing his math, bent over it all careful. He's 15 but he does a college calculus class, and even though he's failing English, Stanford's gonna take him for free 'cause of some project he did. Mamma and Papi's proud of him, 'cause he ain't gonna have to haul garbage like Angelo and he ain't a girl like me.

Celestina was sitting next to him, looking like she was trying to steal a watermelon by hiding it under her shirt. Her dad, this fat Puerto Rican, was gonna shoot Lorenzo, and then him and Papi got into a fight in the park and got arrested, but now they friends 'cause Lorenzo's gonna leave and be rich like Benny's parents.

"*Hola, chica,*" Celestina said. She didn't say nothing to Benny, 'cause she hates him for being white and rich and cold. Most people just think my family's Mexican, 'cause Sicilians are so dark.

"Hi," I mumbled, heading for the kitchen.

Angelo came in and pulled my hair. "Hey, runt. Hey, Benny."

"Ow! Fuck off!" I cried, rubbing my scalp. "What do you want?"

"Some serious shit's gonna go down this week, okay, *Bambolina?*" He pinched my cheek and thought he was being nice, but it left a bruise. His voice was kinda joking, but his eyes was dead serious.

"Yeah, get lost," I said. "And don't call me that." He tweaked my nose hard and I swiped at him with my fist.

"Quit it," Lorenzo snapped. "Leave Annie alone, and shut up while you're at it. I'm doing homework."

"*Hai qualche problema? Ti prendo a sberle ...*" Nonna sounded real pissed from her bedroom, so we all shut the Hell up. She's old, but she can hit hard. One time, she even smacked Benny for looking at her the way he looks at his parents.

"Why you gotta be that way?" I whispered to Angelo.

"What's wrong? Don't want to look bad in front of Benny?" He was smiling, but it was a mean smile.

"Shut up."

"Aw, he your boyfriend now?"

My face was red. "He ain't!" I thought of the Siamese twins.

Angelo looked at Benny seriously. His eyes are hot whiskey, and Benny couldn't freeze 'em. "You better not be. Annie ain't a stupid, fat slut like the other girls in our building, you got it?"

There's me, Fran Goldstein, Maria Sánchez Castro, and Cassy López de Victoria, and I'm the only one who ain't been knocked up before. I also ain't never been alone with a boy. I was always alone with Benny, but I ain't been *alone* with him. We ain't like that. I ain't like that.

"I seem to have a higher opinion of her than you do, Angelo." His voice froze the worm in my guts; it was getting hypothermia.

"Shit, listen to this motherfucker, acting all tough." Angelo pulled on the bill of his baseball cap, tugging it down towards his eyebrows. He always does that when he wants to look tough.

"I don't have an Oedipus complex."

Angelo stared at him and I giggled.

"What? What you laughin' at?" Angelo was pissed.

"Shit, 'cause Oedipus slept with his mom, and Benny don't—so he ain't a motherfucker," I said, giggling more. Benny smiled, barely.

Angelo turned red and I thought he was gonna be the first kid to lay a hand on Benny. I couldn't let that happen, so I threw my body into his. Me and him went down, sister on top of brother, and I said, "No, ya don't!"

Angelo cried out 'cause I slipped and my knee went into his crotch.

"Hey! *Dai!*" Lorenzo yelled, jumping up and sending Celestina into a disgruntled stream of Spanish. He picked me up easy—he was only two years older, but I was little for my age—and clamped his hand over my mouth. "Both of ya! Shut up unless you wanna wake up Nonna again!"

"What the fuck?" The voice was hotter than Angelo's eyes. We all stopped what we was doing and turned at once to look at Papi, standing in the door, his jumpsuit dirty and stinking, his white hair a cloud floating 'round his mountainous, dark face.

"We was just playing, Papi," Lorenzo assured him.

"You two—go home." Celestina stood up and waddled to the door, but Benny hesitated where he was. He looked at me.

"See you tomorrow," I told him stiffly from Lorenzo's arms, and he left, looking like he didn't wanna go.

It was like always, you know. We was bad, so Papi smacked us all good, and I bit him like I usually do, so I got an extra smack.

"You'll learn to love your brothers!" he yelled, swearing and hopping to one side like the black tiles in the kitchen was lava and the white ones was safe. He shook his hand 'cause it was bleeding and had teeth marks in it.

"I love 'em!" I yelled, shocked. Shit, just 'cause you hit your brother in the privates don't mean you don't love him.

He didn't believe me, 'cause he knocked my head against the icebox and sent us to bed without dinner. On the way, Angelo pinched my cheek in the same bruised spot.

"Hear that back there? Annie say she loves us." Angelo was grinning. I took a swipe at him and Lorenzo grabbed my hand.

"*Hey, hey!*" Lorenzo whispered. "*Dai, dai!*"

"Shit, who put you in charge?" Angelo reached for his hat, but Lorenzo took it first. His hand fell, empty.

"You wanna get knocked in the face again?" Lorenzo asked, staring us both down.

"Fuck, whatever," Angelo muttered. He was older than Lorenzo, but he acted younger. He touched his head like he didn't know what to do, and then smacked me on the cheek, and I would've hit him 'cept Lorenzo was still holding onto me. Lorenzo always gotta get in the way.

They went to their room and I went and climbed into bed with Nonna.

When I was staring at the acid-washed Jesus and the Mussolini, I was thinking. Both their faces was pale in the dark, lit by the votive burning under Jesus, and I decided I wanted to be like Mussolini, not Jesus. He never would've let no one smack him in his mouth for nothing. What'd Jesus get for listening to His Dad? His eyes was looking at me, gentle and loving in that awful face, and saying, "No, Annunziata," but my lip was fat and stinging and there was dried blood in my hair, so I decided that was it. No more.

I rolled over and saw Angelo climbing down the fire escape. We was staring at each other, then he pulled down the bill of his Yankees cap and put his finger against his mouth. It wasn't the first time I saw him do it, but it was the first time I saw something tucked in the front of his sagging pants. My guts squirmed and I just kept staring until he left.

Angelo wasn't like Jesus *or* Mussolini; he wasn't no one.

♦

The next day, *I* went and got *Benny*. Took me a while to walk down there, so I had to leave before ten. My teachers never looked for me before class, 'cause they trust me to be in class or doing something for a teacher, but they were wrong for once. I was leaving through the front doors when Lorenzo caught me.

"Hey, where you going?"

"Somewhere."

"Annie, you don't cut." He was holding a pink backpack with a heart on the end of the zipper. I looked for Celestina, and she was coming out of the bathroom with fresh lip gloss on. She waddled over.

"I gotta go see someone." If it was Angelo, I would've just left, or maybe kicked him and left.

"Only person you go see is *Benny, Chica*." Celestina rubbed her belly.

"You ain't going to class, are you?" Lorenzo looked kinda pissed, but only 'cause he was holding a pink backpack and he knew I was gonna leave after he did, and he couldn't do nothing 'bout either thing.

"I ain't." I stuck my chin out so he knew I meant it.

Some older kid in the ninth grade pushed past me, laughing and pulling up his falling pants as he went out the door with his friends. I went after them, and I heard Lorenzo's "*Dai!*" at my back.

I don't have no money to waste on a bus, so I got there just when his class was getting out. I never saw so many kids looking like Mormons in my whole life. When Benny came out of that school that looked like a church, he was talking with some other kids, and he was *laughing*.

For some reason, I never thought Benny had no other friends, and it made me feel funny, like I either had to run up and grab Benny or run away. I was mad, sorta, but not like when Angelo pinches me, mad like maybe I wanted to cry, 'cept I ain't the type for crying and I couldn't make myself move, so I just stood there.

Benny didn't really look surprised or nothing when he saw me. He just raised a dark eyebrow and said, "Annie, you must have walked a long way."

His friends looked at me. This one girl smiled nice and friendly and so did this fat kid, but there was another boy who laughed when he saw me. I was pissed, but I just glared.

"I'm going home," Benny told them, and without saying no more goodbyes than that, he started to walk and I walked with him. He glanced at me, like he knew something. "They aren't my friends."

It don't matter if they was his friends, 'cause as soon as we got back to the plant, there wasn't no one else that mattered anyway.

"I noticed it was glowing this morning," I told him helpfully, and soon as I said it, he looked at it like he noticed for the first time. It don't shed no light exactly, but it just looked bright from the inside, so you could see all the veins and little white hairs. When we touched it, it was warm, and Benny examined it as careful as always, pressing against it 'til we could see the bones in his fingers.

I didn't go home 'til late, and Nonna and Papi was swearing 'bout how Angelo wasn't there, and Mamma was on her knees with a rosary, which is how she spent most of her free time, seemed like.

"One of you better know where he is!" Papi screamed at us. He slammed his fist on the table, then yelled 'cause it was the hand where I bit him. I laughed at him, so I didn't get no dinner again.

I went to bed early and didn't have nothing to look at 'cept my old roommates. I told Mussolini not to worry, 'cause I didn't forget. That Jesus looked sadder than ever.

♦

Today, I say to Benny, "We gonna climb it."

"What? Annie, do you really think we should?" He's surprised and I feel proud. I know he's been wanting to do it all along, but he was waiting for me.

"Yeah. Look: people can't see it, so if we're on it, they shouldn't see us." I'm sure. There's nothing I want more than for Benny and me to be the only two people who can see each other. Just for a while.

He touches my mouth right where it's split, right where nothing but a film of dry blood's holding it together, and it hurts, but it's so good. He never touches no one, and I'm ready to confess my whole heart to him and run away with him to get married and join a circus where he'll be a lion tamer and I'll be a trick rider. I never saw a real horse, but I know I'd be a natural.

But he turns away to look at the plant.

"Okay," he says. "I'll go first, and if it seems okay, I'll come down in a few minutes and get you."

I nod, but I'm sorta worried 'bout Benny going up by himself. He's pretty and soft, and if there's a giant up there, it's gonna tear off his head. But then he looks at me, smiles. Ain't no way no one could ever rip his head off, not even Mussolini. He just gotta look at 'em with them eyes, and they won't be able to do nothing to him, like the rest of the people he meets.

I ask him if he needs a boost, but he looks offended and wraps his arms 'round the plant, one foot on a shoot thick as Angelo's bicep. Then he goes up.

I watch him go up and up 'til he's in the clouds, and then I watch for an hour. Two. Three. I sit down in the street, my back against the plant. Four.

It starts getting dark, and my guts feel wiggly. There's something wrong. I stand up, look up and down and left and right. No Benny, but Angelo's running at me like his ass is on fire.

"Annie!" He plows me over, knocks me down so hard that my skull cracks and echoes in my brain. He's on top of me, holding me down, and someone's shooting a gun. I'm afraid, but my skull's still echoing, squishing against my brain, and I can't say nothing.

"Annie, fuck! Annie, I *told* ya, I *told* ya!" The sound rattles my brain, *squish*, knocking it free, a memory oozing out from a big vein: *Some serious shit's gonna go down this week.* The bruise on my cheek aches where Angelo pinched me.

"Benny," I whimper.

"Fuck, Benny's here too?" Angelo gets up and raises his gun, looking 'round.

"Why *you* here?" I wanna know.

"Them fucking niggers are in our neighborhood, so me and the other—"

"Stop!" I cry, closing my eyes real tight. This ain't how it's supposed to be, and all I can do is lay there under Angelo when the guns go off again. Somewhere, some boys are yelling.

"*Where's Benny?*" Angelo screams, his nose pressed into my cheek, his breath and spit on my face, in my mouth. When I can see his eyes again, they're hotter than I ever saw before.

My eyes roll back, looking up at the sky, and Angelo looks up too. He smashes his hand against my mouth and it tastes like salt and dirty metal. I gag and gasp on his fingers, and when he shoots the gun, I feel the impact through his body on mine.

I look up, searching for Benny, wanting him to stay wherever he is, and try to tell someone that I'm sorry for wanting to be Mussolini when Angelo gets his hand out of my mouth. I cough and almost puke.

Annunciation

"Shut the fuck up, Annie! You wanna die?" Angelo shoots again, rocking my whole body.

From my back, I see Benny falling fast, a bright light out of the clouds. Soaring down, he's Lucifer, the most beautiful thing I ever saw, and tears leak from my eyes. He gathers speed, like a comet, and then stops above the ground. He's wearing the moon on his beautiful white forehead and there's stars in his hair. I'm crying.

Angelo yells and drops to the asphalt. Blood sprays silver out of Benny's chest, onto my face and lips. I scream, leap up and crawl over to where he's laying, my head near exploding from trying,

His blood's turning red, now black.

"Annie," he breathes, silver and black and red all spilling out of his mouth.

"No, Benny," I mouth, and he touches my cheek. I'm screaming and my heart's dying in my chest with every ragged breath he sucks in.

He closes his eyes and don't move, and I try to push them open. He ain't glowing no more, the plant ain't glowing no more. He flickers like the broken light in the school gym, and dies.

I stand up, lost, looking for the plant 'cause I know it's gonna help, but it ain't there. I run over to where it was, hands raised upward, but I don't see nothing. I fall down and crack my knees on the pavement, scraping at the asphalt with my nails, but it ain't there.

"*Dai*, Annie!" I look up in time to see Lorenzo take a bullet in the arm for me. I dunno when he got here. Why he don't stay inside? He crumples on the ground like a used grocery bag and I crawl over to him. I hold his head and he cries in my lap, 'cause we both see it in the sky, I know we do: Jesus and Mussolini are taunting me, God's Son riding by on a circus horse, and Il Duce cracking a whip at a lion.

Waiting for Dawn
by M. James Bizzell

He woke violently, gasping for air, emerging from the velvet dark in confusion. Static spots, the technicolored pixels so familiar from four-a.m. wakings, peeled away in animated clusters. Something tugged at his half-woken reality: a dream. He couldn't remember the details. Something easy, something bad. The nightmares were becoming more present, or at least more lasting. It left him feeling off, settling in an odd position within him, taking up residence in the remote hours.

The effects of sleep apnea were jarring, especially on such quiet nights, from silence to panting terror, the greedy intake of air both confusing and euphoric. He heard nothing in the space beyond the walls of his huddled bedroom, not even the distant hum of overnight trucking. The episodes happened almost every night, every couple of hours. Wake up. Breathe. Wait for your heart to slow and your nerves to calm. Stop shaking. Go back to sleep. It was a constant and gripping fear, a suffocation in empty air—the demon on his chest while he slept.

He felt his wife lying next to him, her rhythmic breathing deep and full, completely undisturbed by his struggle. She had perhaps gotten used to it, but was a deep sleeper in any case. They had made love tonight after she had returned home from a lengthy business trip. It was something they had needed or wanted, probably both. A reward for taking care of the girls while she was away. Parenting had perks.

Despite everything, despite his wife's contented sleep and the warmth of their bed, he was worried. A pervasive feeling had sunk its barbs into his languishing domesticity. The house was quiet. Possibly some remnant of his unborn dream lying buried like a shard within him. Living on their own stretch of land made the wind that blew and filled the house a regular occurrence; it was usually relaxing, but its ethereal noise was absent now. The exclusion shifted the atmosphere in their home a fraction of a degree. Nothing moved in the sallow scenery beyond their home. He could not even hear the clocks ticking from their sentry positions along the walls.

Something was wrong—unexplained and irrational, but very real, nonetheless—a twinge in the forgotten corners of his mind, the vestigial space of prehistory that alerted proto-humans to the predators that owned the night. He had felt this way before, when he was alone, but never, never, with his wife home and his daughters just down the hall, sleeping in their princess-pillowed and punk-postered beds.

He slid out from the warmth of the high thread-counts with deliberate slowness, afraid to disturb the queer stillness. He reached down under the bed and pulled out a revolver locked in a small safe that had been nearly forgotten behind a pile of Poe and Hawthorne. It took him a few tries to work the lock. The gun had been a gift from his father, and it had sat dormant for over five years, collecting dust and the faded memories of an old man. In his hand, the cold metal and the feel of the time-worn wood made him calmer—not safer, but more able. It was always loaded, a concession to the world that they endured.

The door to their bedroom stood open. They didn't close it when the girls were home. One of the first tricks he had learned as a parent was to leave the door open; you never knew when someone would need something.

Light flickered from down the hall and he felt a cold kernel of fear build in his stomach. Lily had left her TV on again; it was as benign as that. He had told her last week how bad that was, how pretty little girls needed their beauty sleep if they wanted to stay pretty. She seemed to take him more seriously after that, but she was still a kid.

Waiting for Dawn

He no longer worried about that stuff with Rachael, it was all boys and emotion now. Let her mother deal with that. At least Lily still thought babies came from kissing. He felt the fear slink away, its tendrils collapsing in the routine of domesticity.

He sighed quietly, his lips turning into a line. He moved towards the door, but kept the revolver in hand. No sense in leaving it in his room, if he had wanted to get it out, then he should keep it out. It felt right, anyway, the cool wood finish fit snugly into the palm of his hand as it had his father's, some 20 years and a badge ago.

Lily's room was at the end of the hall, farthest from the stairs. He passed by Rachael's room on the way. Her door was shut and would be barred if she had her way. That room was her sanctuary, and he supposed all 15-year-olds needed one. He had sure as Hell needed a place away from his own parents when he was her age.

He placed his free hand on Rachel's door and shut his eyes tight. He really wished he hadn't. Maybe his strange sleep had stirred some specters from the past, but the memories themselves were very real. His dad hadn't lived long enough to make up for all those teenage years, never really got to see his son as an adult. His mother still sometimes cried when she saw him, he bore that much resemblance to the old man. He had remained distant after college and that had been a mistake. Rachael would come around—kids always did—and he had plenty of time left to be the good guy.

He moved away from his eldest daughter's room and padded across the hardwood floor. It was always cold this time of year, but Steph preferred it to carpet, and if the woman wanted wood floors, she got them. She was king of this castle; she paid the bills, he raised the kids. It worked for them in a 21st-century kind of way. His grandfather, a World War veteran who had received two Purple Hearts and a Bronze Star, would have been sick to see it.

He passed by the office. That door was never open, but it was tonight. When she was at home, Stephanie would sit in there for hours, calling execs and making travel plans while he made dinner and sat through the newest and most compelling episode of whatever sophomoric drivel Lily had found. He didn't mind it really; he loved his wife and he loved the girls, but sometimes he craved a place safe from the prepubescent antics of child stars.

Lily was asleep in the floor in front of her bed, curled up with a blanket twisted around in her arms. The girl seemed to travel when she slept, just like her father. He set the revolver down on her dresser, next to what must have been the largest collection of stuffed animals in the known world, and picked her up carefully, his knees popping as he stood.

She felt weightless in his arms, like a doll, and as much as he teased her about it, she looked like one. Her blonde curls framed her pink face, and her blue eyes—closed now—could light up a room. He was sure she would break hearts when she was Rachael's age, and he was just as sure that he would be waiting on the porch with a fully-loaded scowl.

He set her down on the bed and covered her with a princess-themed comforter. She was a princess, his little princess, and he felt whole. But he felt old, too. Barely 40 and falling apart. He should have treated his youth as a gift. His father had warned him about it, but he wouldn't listen. Boys had to prove that they were men all the time, lest anyone forget.

He grabbed his gun on the way out and shut Lily's door. There was something calming about doing that. Shutting doors meant safety, and in a house full of women, safety was the name of the game.

He walked back to the master bedroom and saw light flicker through the doorway. Someone had moved in front of the porch light that shined in from outside. Stephanie had woken up. He held the gun down beside his leg and moved to the room more quickly. It would be hard to explain its presence to his wife when he could hardly explain it to himself. Despite the assurance of such a normal and regular act, he was frightened. His heart rate had spiked, and he could feel the adrenaline seeping into him. He fought to steady his breathing, but it was a losing battle. Everything was fine. Steph had gotten up to use the bathroom, and when he went in, he would see the light on from underneath the door. Everything was fine.

Flick. Something moved in front of the light again—slower, more deliberate. He could feel his face tightening, the skin stretching over his skull. He pulled the gun up slowly, his hand gripping it like iron. He pushed the door open and winced as it hit the wall.

What he saw in the room was familiar and quiet. The bed, off to his right, lay in darkness, and he could see his wife laying there, still sleeping. Nothing moved within the room; it was dark and still. His eyes darted around the room, taking everything in with heightened sensitivity. Nothing. Empty and whole.

The light from the porch outside bathed the room in a sort of dim glow, a blue ether that was reserved for the center of the room only. Stephanie had left the blinds open. She liked to watch the rain fall, and they had sat there together tonight, but he always wanted them closed afterward. Something moved in front of the light again, cutting off the ethereal glow in the room. His eyes shot up and he felt his heart snag on something inside. On the balcony, silhouetted by the porch light, stood a man.

He drew the gun up clumsily before realizing the man was standing with his back to him under the glow of the light. His head was shaved and he appeared to be wearing a neon T-shirt, the kind of shirt he expected to see on one of his daughter's friends.

Probably a fucking kid looking for Rachael. He wanted to shoot the dumb shit. He couldn't believe the crap kids pulled now. He had never tried to sneak into someone's house; that was the height of idiocy. The kid had probably tried climbing the balcony to look for his daughter, but he was going to find a foot up his ass if he ever stepped on his property again.

He felt the fear slide away, leaving a slick residue of rage. All that remained was anger. Anger for the stupid kid scaring the shit out of him.

The fucking nerve. He moved toward the double doors with the gun still in his hand, oblivious to the fact that he wasn't wearing anything over his underwear. He pushed open the door and closed it behind him. It was best to not let his wife see him threatening minors.

"Hey, buddy. Turn around." His voice had a familiar edge in it. He never talked to his wife or daughters like that. "The voice," as Rachael called it, was reserved for assholes and her friends—synonymous, as far as he was concerned.

The kid's head jerked up, but he didn't turn around. The kid looked a lot older than he was expecting, but it could be the soft glow coming from below the deck boards, filling in the figure with deep shadows. He actually looked like he could be 30, with the softness of excess fat hanging from his hips and exposed shoulders. He really didn't understand kids anymore. Their smoking and drinking would make them 60 by the time they were actually 30.

"Listen, I don't want you coming around here, especially not at night. I could have fucking shot you, kid. Get off my property and don't come around Rachael anymore, or I swear to God, I'll call the police." He moved to grab the kid. The asshole would look at him; he deserved respect.

The kid's head whipped around. He was at least 30, there was no mistaking it. His face was coarse with a few days' worth of stubble and his head wasn't shaved, he was bald. The man's eyes were boring holes into him, too. They weren't normal, they were too intense. Then he noticed the blood.

It was everywhere. On the man's shirt, on his hands, in his mouth. Slippery blood covering him. There was also something lying at his feet, a mutilated corpse, its hair matted over what remained of the body: Alexander, their five year-old German shepherd. The dog had been Lily's gift at age three, and he was staring at what remained of the dog, his dog.

He jerked the revolver up just as the man fell on him with bloodstained hands. He was stronger than he looked, and much faster. The man's hands tore into him like knives, taking ragged clumps of flesh out of his body with every frenetic blow. The bald man cut into him like a ragged knife, burning everything he touched. It was all he could do to cover his eyes and kick out with a frantic movement.

The blood-soaked man stumbled back and let out a cry that sounded far less than human. The man was sick, that much was clear. He pointed the gun at the man's chest and fired twice in quick succession, double-action, without pulling back the hammer. The first round hit its mark, more or less, but the second sailed wide of the target and clipped the bald man on his forehead. The bullet ripped across the skin, exposing the skull and spraying flesh across the deck. The kick had been greater than he expected, but the surprise of actually firing the weapon in anger was more deafening than the sudden noise.

The bald man slumped down against the rail, smearing a crimson streak across the manicured white wood. He had stopped moving forward, but his eyes never lost their intense glare. His body was failing him, but he still clawed at the open air, howling as he did so.

He squeezed off another round at the man's head, hitting him in the bridge of the nose. The face caved in under the impact, trickling the blood that remained, and the bald man went still with that horrid glare fixed to his face.

He rose quickly from the gore all around him. His dog was dead, he was bleeding from his shoulder and chest, and he had shot and killed a man. Their blood mixed freely on the deck where they held summer barbeques with his mother.

His eyes snapped back to the double doors just as his wife opened them, her face a mask of shock and confusion.

"Mark? I think I heard—" She cut off midsentence, no doubt seeing the blood.

"Steph, sweetie, go inside and get the girls. It's not safe out here."

"What is that? You're bleeding, you're bleeding, Mark!"

Her tone was winding up, shifting higher, leaving the ground below. His mind was racing. The girls would have woken up. There were two bodies on his balcony and his daughters were waking up. They couldn't see this. They couldn't see him like this.

Mark threw down the revolver and wiped his hands on his undershirt, but they only came away with more blood. He felt sick; he was losing blood, sure, but he had killed a man. It was self-defense—they had to see that. The police would be on their way soon, there would be an investigation, and his family would see him covered in blood—

"Mark, look at me!"

She was screaming now, her blue eyes—so much like Lily's—were sharp and horrified. He had drifted off, lost somewhere in his head. He had to get her back inside, away from what would undoubtedly be called a murder.

Mark extended his arms, pushing her back with soothing noises.

"Baby, go inside. He just came at me. I think … I think he killed Alexander. Honey, no, stop. We need to get the girls, something wasn't right with him. I think he was sick." He led her away from the blood with as much grace as he could muster.

She wouldn't touch him, and he thought he could feel that sane cold look in his own eyes. He was a murderer.

He was shaking. The adrenaline spike that had filled him seconds before dumped him down, made him feel hollow and cold.

Stephanie shrank back into the house. Shrank. She was not a tall woman, but she could make her presence felt in any situation. Not once had she ever been afraid of him, but there, he could see it. She was more than afraid, she was terrified and confused and distant all at once. The girls would not see him like this.

"Get me a shirt, Stephanie. I need you to call the police and get me a clean shirt. Get the girls and head downstairs, they don't need to see this."

It surprised him just how level his voice was. He had gunned down another human being and he was carrying on like he had just returned from the store.

♦

Stephanie set down the phone for the fifth time. The girls sat huddled across from her, not looking at him. Sometimes Rachael would glance up quickly, but her eyes would find the floor again before he could make eye contact and reassure her. They feared him, too. Not so much Lily, she really didn't understand what was going on—she just kept screaming for the dead dog and crying. He had tried to hug her then, but Stephanie gave him a look that told him that in no uncertain terms would he be allowed to touch his daughter.

The line was busy. 911 was busy. The thought roiled within him. Something was going on. He felt that same slick feeling he had when he woke. He had not imagined it.

Mark looked up at Stephanie. Her head was in her hands, her long, dark hair falling around her face.

"He was sick, Steph. He tried to kill me."

"Shut up, just shut up. I can't hear this. The girls don't need to hear this."

"Sweetie, please. Don't do this."

Now he could feel the fear creeping into his voice. She was distancing herself from him. She was just as scared as he was, if not more so. Her husband had just killed a man, and now only a busy tone reached them through the phone.

Lily flipped on the TV and the silence stretched on, punctured only by the sobs of his wife and youngest daughter. The den filled with an ether-blue glow and Mark could see Rachael looking at him again.

He rose quietly and sat beside his wife. He pulled her close, and if she stiffened at first, it melted away in a heartbeat. He was the same man she had made love to a few hours ago, the father of her children. She had to see that.

Stephanie began to sob quietly, her head resting against his bruised and bloodied chest. She had bandaged what she could, but he could feel his wounds burning with infection through his clothes.

"I don't want you to go. I need you."

It was muffled against his chest, but he could hear her. The words were just for him, and he was grateful for that. He would do what he must, but he would not abandon his family. Tears trickled down his face, unchecked.

Lily came up to him and stuck her face in front of his.

"Why isn't the TV working, Daddy?"

Mark looked up and touched his daughter's tiny face.

"It's working, sweet girl, you just have to change the channel." He took the remote from her and tried toggling to something other than the news.

"I did, Daddy. It's on every channel."

He stared at the television for a few stunned seconds before unmuting it. There was a middle-aged man with a microphone and an ear-piece shouting to be heard over the whirl of sirens.

"—officials have cordoned off the area, do not go into the city. Do not go into the city."

He leaned forward despite the discomfort he felt in his chest. There it was, that flood of fear, the culmination of the entire uneasy night. His body tingled; it felt like staring into the mouth of Hell. Something was going on, and it displaced something essential within him.

"I don't think the cops are coming, dad," Rachael finally spoke.

Waiting for Dawn

He looked up at his eldest and smiled bitterly in the dim glow of the television that breached the darkness.

"No, baby, I don't think they are."

The Other End of the Lake

by Dara Marquardt

I don't remember much about my death. I don't even think of it very often. At first, it was all I could think of, but that only lasted a little while. Now, I know that I'm dead. There's no sense rehashing it.

What I really recall is the white. Sometimes I think about it as I watch him sleep. I think of the blinding white light and wonder if that's where heaven comes from. There were slices of light that night, and they remain sharp, like cut stone. The white of headlights dancing off the rim of the steering wheel. The scattered diamonds of rain on the windshield. The wipers as they scrape against glass. The chrome door handle shining as I put the key in the lock. The glow of the stereo as I turned the knob.

I remember looking at Jane. She was burning as she sat by the hospital bed. She was burning as she'd burned in a field of golden green the first time I saw her. Her mouth a clever smile, her eyes like two secrets, her skin like white honey. She was beautiful then, with her blonde hair down and tree shadows hiding the edges of her cheeks. And she was beautiful in that T-shirt she slept in, sweatpants on, our daughter on her lap.

She was beautiful when I died. I don't think I'll forget that.

It was hard at first, to look at things. Everything was very bright. Jane, maybe because I loved her, love her still, was the brightest. But our daughter was bright, too. I remember wanting, needing, to reach out and touch her cheek. To feel the fine strands of her brown hair. To be near her. To feel the warmth of the light burning through her.

I remember raising my hand to brush away the strings of pearl-sized tears shimmering down Jane's face, when Angie started crying. I withdrew my hand, amazed at the sound, the sound coming from her toothy mouth. I remember the pain of each of those teeth. I remember the sticky feel of teething gel as I rubbed it on her gums. I remember the weight of her warm, snuggly body in the crook of my arm as I fried eggs at four in the morning. I remember how she looked when she took her first breath.

I did not reach for her again.

When my wife and daughter left the hospital room, the light went with them. And when the light came again, I could no longer find them.

Now I am too weak to look. And if I found them, I think Angie would cry.

This boy, I found him by accident. Really, I found him when he carried the flowers. Tiger lilies. A full, bursting orange bouquet of tiger lilies. They were so big they spilled over his arms like tangerine jewels, tiny grains of pollen fluttering to his heels.

He was following his mother and I followed him. They went to a room down a very long hall and I waited in the doorway, unsure of the gray man lying in bed. Did he look gray to them? Could they see the gray looming, not outside him like a caul, but from within him like a pulse? I could. I could.

I stood in the doorway, the scent of tiger lilies strong and high, watching as the boy put the flowers in a plastic cup, and his mother sat in a chair and held the gray man's hand.

The mother was bright, but not as bright as Angie and nowhere near as bright as Jane. But she had a little light. It flickered off her rings when she combed her fingers through her hair. It shined off her teeth when she talked. It spilled from her lips like Angie's startled cry when I reached to touch her. Her voice was the sound of a quiet ribbon drawn through silver hoops.

The boy had light, too.

The Other End of the Lake

When they left the room, I followed. I followed through the hall. We passed other gray people, some in wheelchairs, some leaning on IV poles as they took cautious steps in apple red non-skid slippers. Some wore doctor badges and others wore the crisp attire of nurses. The fluorescent tubes suspended above us like a glass intestinal tract seemed to dim things instead of illuminating them. They buzzed inside my head.

I think it was then that I realized I was fading. I was soaking into the linoleum floors like dirt into porous grout. I was folding into the cinder-block walls like dew slipping into the tiny mouths of flat leaves. Soon I would be nothing. I would be the carbon in the paint. I would be the water running down the cold, aluminum drains. I would cease.

Outside was overwhelming. It was a chaotic twist of colors and gray, of streaks of shadow and trembles of movement. I tried to look all around all at once, my eyes bulging and thoughts disjointed. I barely made it to their car. I felt not a sense of relief when the boy hopped in the backseat and closed the door, but a sense of stalled obliteration. He played a handheld game and laughed.

The mother drove and the boy wore his seatbelt. They talked a little, but I can't say what it was about. I closed my eyes because the city scared me. It was like no city I had ever seen. All the happenings happened too fast. Pedestrians seemed to jet from corner to corner, streetlights flickered like idiot strobes, the cars growled and grinned.

And the boy radiated with light.

I wanted to put my hand on his. To be near that light. To feel its warmth and in it know the ache of breath in pink lungs. To know the firing crash of synapses snapping in the brain. To feel the roll of a tongue across the jagged pickets of teeth as the mouth made words.

But I did not. I was still too afraid. Afraid, maybe, that he would cry like Angie had cried. That I would see not the mother jerking in her seat, twisting her neck to see what was wrong with her son, but

Jane clutching Angie, clutching our daughter as if her mother's arms held her back from the edge of a frothing abyss.

The abyss is me.

It's when I sit next to him on the swing set out back that I think of all the things I did. Sometimes it feels I did so many things that I did nothing at all. I answered phone calls and sent emails. I took home paychecks and I bought groceries. I worked on the car when it needed it and I drank beer when I didn't want it. There were too many nights I fell asleep without kissing my wife goodnight. There were too many mornings when I was cranky without reason. There were good things, too, and I'd like to say I long for them now.

I long for the edges of Jane's T-shirt dancing against her thighs as she made breakfast on Saturdays. I long for the feel of her hair brushing against my face as we sat on a bench at the park and watched Angie toddle around the seesaw. I miss the smooth feel of Angie's baby feet against my cheeks as I pretended to eat her toes.

And I do miss these things. But I miss the light more. I miss the light more.

Sometimes when I lie on the boy's floor as he dreams in his bed, tucked under the quilt of Spiderman, his nightlight glowing—but duller than he glows—I wonder if this is hurting him. I wish I could say this thought worries me, but it does not.

His eyes seem darker. His skin seems lighter. He plays at his friends' houses less often. He regularly picks at his dinner, shifting it around his plate like front-loaders shift dirt mounds at elaborate construction sites.

I wonder if the boy is dying.

♦

His mother is edgy. Twice in the past week, she yelled at him in the morning, once with only one side of her face made up. For a moment, she was a monster with half a face, one half painted with a perfect mask, the other naked and ugly. I think the boy was afraid.

I wonder if he can feel me sitting on the swing next to him. He comes outside most days, as if the fall sunlight will magically invigorate him, like he's a misfiring solar cell, just on the verge of collecting the charge he so desperately needs.

I've begun to share my sleep with him. That's how I think of it. I'm not entirely sure what we're doing, but he and I are together in the depths of his dreams.

In all of them, we are standing on opposite sides of a mirror-calm lake. The water is the gray steel of northern rain in cold winter. It is the gunmetal color of my car before it went off the road. It is the calm on Jane's face as the doctor's sliced her uterus open and pulled from her body our Angela June.

There is a wind in this dream and the dust is heavy and thick. From my side of the lake, I can see his hair blow. I can see the brown of his eyes shine. I can feel the warmth coming from his skin and I want to walk across the water.

♦

I was unsure if he recalled these dreams. Today, I got my answer. I follow him to school now. I close my eyes on the school bus because the city still scares me. I'll never get used to it. Not like this. Ginny Porter shoots him worried glances and tucks her elbows into her ribs when he walks by. She doesn't seem to like him, but when I first met the boy, he shared a package of chocolate covered pretzels with her at recess. Twice.

The teacher calls on him, but her mouth is pinched when she says his name. Sometimes he looks out the window for a long time. Sometimes he stays in his seat after the lunch bell rings. Once, he made a mess in his pants and wept in the bathroom until someone came to look for him. I'm not sure, but I think the school called his mother.

Today he drew me. I'm guessing it was me. I recognized the lake. He's a very talented artist.

For our second wedding anniversary, Jane bought me a hat. It was more of a joke than anything, and it pleased her to the moon when I actually wore it. I don't think I took it off that entire summer. It was tan with a black band around it, an old-timey fedora she found at one of the thrift stores where she was always spending our "fun cash." A red feather tucked into the end of it, just like an old-fashioned gangster. I wore it cocked over my left eye. I remember her wearing it a few times. That and nothing else.

The boy drew the lake. He used three shades of blue and three shades of gray to get the water just right. The edges of it were crisp in our dream and crisp in his drawing. In his artwork, I cannot see him. I can see only me. I stand at the end of the lake. I am tall, as I always was. My shoulders are like two slabs of black clay. In his art, I am a shadow. I wear a tilted hat with a red feather tucked into the brim.

I feel as if I'm shrinking. Growing not thinner, but smaller. I feel sometimes, usually in the crisp silence of late, late night, that I am small enough to be ingested, that the boy, if he breathes deep enough, might lift me from my spot on the floor and take me into his lungs, take me into the light. My mind tingles with this and I lay silently, willing it to happen. Waiting on the cold, unforgiving wood of his bedroom floor while he sleeps beneath his blanket, for him to inhale me. To breathe me. To induct me into the light that I cannot stop craving.

Sometimes at night, I run my fingers against the mop of his hair. Sometimes thoughts of Angie try to invade then. I think of her as an infant, waking for no reason from the warm nest of her crib, her mouth a red inferno, screams echoing off the yellow walls. I think of her then, my tiny infant daughter, glowing with light. And if these thoughts will not retreat, I lie down again because I am too ill with a mix of unease and sheer starvation to do anything else.

When I sleep, it is deep and cumbersome. It's like a heavy coat on a warm summer night. It cloys but it protects, and I feel myself standing on my end of the lake. This is a lake I can reach only in these deep dreams. It is a lake the boy has come to, but I don't know how he found it. In this place, we are alone and the world is a black fist. We are two creatures trapped in a stint.

The dust is less and less each time I dream. The night is poked with needles and the veins of the universe hemorrhage gold. I can see him standing on his end. I can see him with the orange bouquet of tiger lilies in his arms. I think when the dust clears, I might be able to walk across the water. I might be able to walk across it.

♦

The boy's mother took him to the doctor. When they pricked his arm, he bled. They checked his iron levels. They listened to the beautiful drum of his heart. I worry for him. I held his hand. I think he held mine back.

There was no school today, so the boy went on a walk. His street is quiet. An old couple lives on the corner and he waved to them, but no one else said hello. We went to a culvert that runs below a street two blocks from his house. It was grassy and stiff with chill. The trees are all nearly bare; only the evergreens are still vibrant. The boy saw a rabbit. It was gray and thin, its eyes like two black rocks.

The sparkle in its eyes was like tiny candles burning in a cave. I think that's why he killed it. I watched him bury the corpse in the dirt. He covered it with a fast food wrapper. I wish I felt bad about this, but I don't.

The walk exhausted me. Tomorrow, there will be school again. We will ride the bus together. I will sit by him—none of the other kids sit near him anymore. His shoelaces will click when the bus goes over bumps. His bag is bare, but on him, it looks heavy. I will close my eyes when we drive through the city because I'm still afraid of all of its monstrous colors and painful speeds. But the boy is not.

I lie on the rug near him, willing myself to shrink, to be small enough to go inside. Thoughts of Jane rocking Angie push at me. I push them back. They remind me of the times we left Angie's room, sleepy and tired, haggard and exhausted, as she settled and we closed the door. These thoughts shove at me and in my ears, there is still an echo of her startled cry. I shove them back.

When I dream, I dream of the lake. I dream of the boy. Somehow only a thread of him is left. The thread. The white rod burning inside him. The boy on the other end of the lake is beautiful and pure and full and new. He is solid and unblemished. All of the vestiges and worry and pettiness have been wiped away, much like winter's first harsh snowfall will strip the land of its superficial marks. He stands with tiger lilies in his hand. Tiny grains of pollen flutter from their orange tips. The needle holes mar the ink of night, golden spires slipping into the sky like a shy universe.

The wind has settled. The night is clear. I adjust my hat and take the first step. I discover the water and it's solid—solid enough to walk across.

Low Prowls The Goblin King

by David Barclay

The room is quiet and still, quiet and still save for The Goblin King, who stands high in the corner on the shelf, the one above the old chest which once upon a time held all of William's worldly things, including The Goblin King himself. Now he stands high in the corner, high in the corner where the wood meets the wall and the shelf brace hangs crooked, the place where the carpenter's nail is bent imperceptibly where it joins the wall and bends the shelf down at the end, ever so slightly.

In the doorway, Tucker Bill Atley stares across the musty threshold at The Goblin King, stares and stares and musters his courage to cross the room.

In two quick strides, he stumbles forward and throws open the drapes, letting the gray Pennsylvania sun into the tiny bedroom. Beside him, the covers lay undisturbed on the bed, the vanity sits closed and locked. All is as he and Alice left it when they closed the room and tucked the key into the nightstand next to their bed, when it had been *their* bed, in the time before.

Tucker knows all of William's toys. He knows the He-Man dolls, the Power Rangers, the hobbits and the dwarves and the orcs. He knows they are sleeping now, piled in the chest in a mishmash of arms and legs and swords, just as he left them. William is gone now, but he left The Goblin King, his favorite, who now stands high in the corner.

The bottle in Tucker's hand rises with gravitational certainty, and the bourbon washes down his throat like warm fire. He snorts. The bedroom key drops from his hand and onto the rug beneath his feet, drops into infinity amongst the endless patterns of spiraling brown and white. The key is lost in an instant, lost like William.

In this moment, Tucker thinks he is too young to be an uncle, too young to be guardian, to have lost the one person in the world who he was sworn to protect. He thinks he is too young to be a drunk. In spite of what he and his friends used to say, 31 is not old, surely not old enough to be damned. And yet here he stands alone, staring high in the corner at the old yellow walls and the crooked shelf where The Goblin King now rests.

The Goblin King stares back, stares down the length of his horny, crooked nose, down the length of his hairy, knobbly chin. His glass eyes shine impetuously in the morning light, his left hand cast out in front of him, cast out accusingly. Upon one finger rests a ring, the coiled image of a serpent eating its own tail. The Ouroboros. The cycle of life and death, the cycle condemning Tucker Bill to repeat each day without his nephew, without his William, with only The Goblin King and a broken promise to keep him company.

I'll protect him, George. As your brother, I swear I will.

Standing in the middle of the room, gazing high into the corner, Tucker has another drink. As the bottle crests his lips, a strange fragment of poetry skirts across his consciousness:

Low comes the wind over roof and eave
Low comes the serpent, the wyrm of ring
Blows the wind through the dry and the dark
Whispering the wiles of the horned king

Tucker is a simple man, a logger from the green hills of the Adirondacks like his father before him and his grandfather before. He is a simple man but not a simpleton; Tucker Bill Atley has the soul of an artist, the curse of an artist. Many a night he has been up with the masters, with Frost, with Stevens, with Eliot, with Yeats. And yet this poem, he knows, this poem is not from any of the tomes on his shelf. Where does it come from? It taunts him, this verse, it makes him feel strange. It makes him feel

"Low," he says to the empty room. "Goddamn low."

And then behind him comes the familiar pitter-patter of footsteps, the sound he knows so well, the sound which he has surely heard a million times now, echoes down the hall, a ghostly reverberation inside his subconscious. Tucker knows it is not real and yet still he turns, turns to the sound of his nephew running down the hall.

"William?" he calls. "William is that you?"

No, of course not. The boy has been gone these three long months, gone like the wind on the cool autumn day on which he disappeared. Tucker was in the backyard when it happened, out in the great green expanse behind the cabin. He had been working on a new sculpture, chainsaw in hand, chipping at the old oak log. The old oak log he planned to sell to Myrtle Hawkens at the antique store on Common Street, once it had been shaped and cut.

In the grass, he had been chipping at the bark, chipping and chipping with the soul of an artist, when Alice had come from the back door yelling William's name. She lives up north with her mother now, Alice does, lives up north in the cold and the dark on the east side of the train tracks in Southrun, far from the cabin. The last time she called was to tell him the cops were moving on, moving on and sending his file to cold cases. William was just a cold case, a dead case, and Tucker Bill needed to find him, to *get off your ass and find him, Bill, find him!*

The Goblin King points to the hallway, points with his accusing hand, and Tucker can take no more. He lunges forward and grabs the toy by the waist. Just then, he hears William's footsteps echoing once more, this time from the basement.

Through no will of his own, Tucker's feet carry him across the hall to the old oak door leading down to the cellar, down to the cellar and the low earthen room beneath the cabin. Smells of mud and concrete drift up the stairs, smells of old wood and old paint and old jars and something else, too, something not quite old but not quite pleasant. Something Tucker can't quite forget even through the liquor haze.

"Uncle Tucky! Uncle Tucky, come and see!" William says.

But William is not there, not really, and Tucker does not want to go and see. He does not want to go and see, and yet he must, because when he hears William's voice and hears the footsteps, he starts to think it all might be a dream, a terrible dream, that he is still in the backyard working on his sculpture, carving the log to sell to Myrtle Hawkens, and little William is not low.

One foot steps down upon the stair.

Careful.

Careful now.

Tucker Bill swerves and sways and has another drink to steady himself. Somewhere above, he can hear the breeze creaking and craning against the old roof, and he can feel that verse, that strange verse, creaking and craning in his mind.

Low comes the wind.

If he knows one thing, Tucker knows he is low, he is *goddamn low*, and he doesn't need a book to tell him. His feet plod down the stairs, and the liquor takes over, and the verse takes over, and he forgets about the third stair from the bottom, the third stair with the loose board, and he goes sprawling.

Tucker crashes to the floor, crashes and cracks and clatters. The bottle rolls from his hand and skirts off into shadow, lost to the darkness.

Tucker finds himself down amongst the cobwebs, amongst the old furniture. Down amongst dirt piles scattered randomly on the floor. He is wet now, bleeding. For a moment he thinks he might be bleeding to death, but it is only a puddle, a large pancake puddle beneath the rusted red pipe with the duct-taped joint, the pipe that hangs crooked, crooked like the shelf in William's room.

For one blissful moment, his head spins and he forgets why he is here. Then the fog clears and he remembers The Goblin King, The Goblin King in his hand. He rises, wet and freezing.

Something wriggles across the floor, and he thinks it is a snake, but it's only a length of rope spilling from a box overturned in the tumble. It is portentous, that rope, long and coiled and knowing, somehow knowing.

Low comes the serpent.

Then Tucker's gaze falls all the way down, and he sees the rug. Another rug with the same spiral patterns as the rug above, the one that always reminds him of the ring, of the snake eating its tail. With one quick motion, Tucker yanks that rug from the floor, yanks it like tape on flesh. With the bottle lost to the dark, he is too sober, far too sober to do what comes next.

Staring at the hole beneath, Tucker thinks how perfect his name is, how apt. Each night he tucked William into bed, tucked him beneath the covers and read to him, not Frost or Eliot, but children's books in a child's tongue. He tucked him in like a father, tucked him in until that moment in the backyard, the moment when William ran up behind him, and Tucker slipped with the chainsaw.

And then Tucker Bill didn't tuck little William into bed but brought him here to the cellar and tucked him into the hole beneath the rug, tucked him low, low, low. Tucked him in before anyone could see.

Gently, he places The Goblin King next to the body of his nephew. William with his favorite toy.

Complete.

Tucker scrapes the piles of earth back into the hole, scrapes and scrapes until the hole is filled. He thinks he is finished, thinks the worst is over, when he gazes into the puddle and sees a shape reflected back. What he should see is a haggard man with a bloody lip, a man with thick, knotted arms and an old Steelers cap and an old steely gaze. An old man of 31.

What he sees instead is a thing with gnarled, green skin. The horny, crooked nose, the hairy, knobbly chin, they are his now. He has become the monster, a king whose kingdom is despair.

When at last he looks away, he sees the rope on the floor, and he knows there is but one fate for monsters, one fate for those who crawl and slither and prowl beneath the earth. One fate for those who kill the only thing in the world they love.

Tucker threads the rope through an eyehook in the ceiling, then wraps the cord around his neck. As he steps up onto a box, he hears William's footsteps, hears him running up the stairs and laughing, laughing. Then he hears the sound of the chainsaw, and the short scream that follows.

"Low," Tucker says.

And drops.

Unfurled

by Kiya Krier

"No home toys at school, Rylan," I said, folding myself into the preschool-sized chair.

He pulled the orange figurine from his pocket. His pants were on backward. Again.

"She's not a toy," he said. "She's a real, live dragon." The model stood, head held high, front foot cocked off Rylan's scabbed palm, little wings unfurled slightly.

"Beautiful. Put the toy in your cubby."

His dark brows drew together. "Ms. Kathy, she doesn't like when people call her that."

I glanced at my watch. Three minutes late. "Of course, just put it away."

I followed Rylan with my eyes as I sang the circle-welcoming song to the rest of the class. His ankles showed between his shoes and pant hems. The scabs were back. If only he would stop picking them.

I skimmed through the calendar, letter of the week, and weather watcher. We moved to the table to glue paper strips in an alternating pattern of yellow and blue. I walked between the two tables crowded with little chairs and swinging shoes. On the table beside Rylan's tray stood his dragon toy.

I stopped. "Rylan, why did you get your toy out?"

"She's not a toy." He smeared a glue stick across a blue strip of paper.

My eyebrow shot up. "How did she get next to your tray?"

He looked at me with those pale eyes. "She got bored in

159

my cubby."

"Nice try. Put her back."

Rylan shrugged. "She won't stay there."

"I suggest she does, or we'll have a problem."

Rylan scooped up the toy and carried her to the cubbies. He placed her carefully on top of his shelf and stood muttering, the hand on his hip seeming too adult for his little frame. Only Rylan would act out an imaginary game so thoroughly.

He walked back to the table, shaking his head. "I told her, but her listening ears are not on today."

"Reminds me of someone I know." I turned to the rest of the class. "If you finished gluing your pattern, put your tray on the drying rack and sit down on the carpet." Chairs screeched out from the tables and children swarmed around the room. Interesting how they always chose the longest possible route to the drying rack.

"Hands to yourself, Liam. Wait your turn, Hayden." From the corner of my eye, I saw something shoot through the air. "Lizzy! We don't throw toys inside." Lizzy's lower lip trembled. *Here we go.*

"I didn't," she protested. To avoid a meltdown, I turned my attention back to the flock of children around the drying rack. My eyes landed on the dragon toy poking out of Rylan's back pocket. *You've got to be kidding.*

"Rylan." His head whipped around, all innocent, big eyes. "The toy," I sighed.

"In my cubby."

"Put her away." He stared at me. "Stop acting like you don't know what I mean. In your pocket." Reaching behind him, he patted at his pocket, fishing out the dragon.

"I told you to stay put." He held the dragon up to his face, eyes crossed. I didn't understand how he found time to get to his cubby. I held out my hand, putting on a stern look. Rylan handed her over, shoulders drooping. "How do you make someone listen when they

Unfurled

don't want to?"

"Figure that out and you can bring a home toy to school every day."

He nodded and bolted to the carpet to join the rest of the class. I placed the toy on the cubby shelves higher than my shoulder. It now crouched low, head almost brushing the shelf, teeth bared. Toys got fancier every year.

"Out of the blocks center," I said to a stray child.

I ducked into the closet, grabbing *Green Eggs and Ham*. When I came out, Rylan's fingers had crept under the hem of his pants.

"Rylan, stop picking." His hand whipped out again, eyes glued to the shelf. "Tyler, we do not lay on our friends. Fingers out of your nose, Beth." The joys of teaching three-year-olds.

I read through the story, skimming over the words, my eyes on the clock more than the book. Somehow we had fallen another four minutes behind schedule. Hopefully it didn't make us late for recess.

Around the time Sam's friend refused to try green eggs and ham in a car, I sent Lizzy to use the bathroom. When she came out, I called Rylan. I worked my way through the circle of squirming kids, then called each of them to grab their jackets. When Rylan left to grab his coat, the dragon toy was crouching on the carpet where he had been sitting.

I dropped *Green Eggs and Ham* to my knees.

"How did you even reach it?" My voice came out higher than I intended. Half the class paused in their scramble for coats. Still oblivious, Rylan continued bobbing away. "Rylan," I snapped. He turned, palms up. I pointed to the offending toy. Infuriatingly, he laughed.

"I don't see what's so funny. You completely ignored my directions." A child had not disrespected me like this in years.

"Ms. Kathy, it wasn't—"

"Stop." I stood up. "I can't stand lying in my class." I swiped the

161

toy off the floor and stalked to the closet. "It stays here for the rest of the day." The lock snapped shut with finality. I exhaled deeply, smoothing my cardigan against my stomach. I walked toward the swarm of kids who had resumed grabbing jackets, swatting at each other and cutting in line.

As I zipped Kelly's coat, a muffled thud sounded from the closet. *I shouldn't have balanced those books on the cleaning bucket this morning.* Then another. And another. Then a loud snap as something large struck the door.

"What's in there?" Liam asked, putting me between himself and the closet. Most of the kids had turned toward the locked door, various stages of terror and excitement on their faces. Someone said something about monsters. Great, how would I explain that to parents? *No, Mr. Scott, I don't know why Liam suddenly fears monsters in the school closet.*

I strode to the door and flung it open.

"What in the world?"

Rainbow-colored feathers and scraps of paper floated to the ground. Plastic bins of supplies which moments before had been stacked on shelves, were dumped across the floor of the closet. Red sand poured from the top shelf in a soft whisper. Shredded books toppled off another shelf at waist level.

There at eye level, the orange dragon stood rampant, claws reaching, mouth open to the sky, wings extended. *Maybe—no.* I shook my head, eyes closed. A dry little hand brushed my fingers.

Odd batches of hair jutted out around Rylan's ears.

"What's going on?" I asked.

"I told you."

"Not possible."

He shrugged, gazing at her. I peeked at the clock. So late. We'd missed half of recess already. I put my free hand over my eyes. I could hear the noise of the class increasing behind me. I needed to do something to end this. I snatched the figurine off the shelf, holding tight. I turned and paused, unsure of what to do with the toy. A shift inside my hand made me jump. The dragon clattered to the ground, the click of plastic on tile bringing me back to reality.

"Careful, Ms. Kathy." Rylan scooped the dragon up and cuddled it to his chest.

"Just," I looked at the class, which had erupted, "don't let me see her again." Not wanting to know what he did with it, I strode away from Rylan and his dragon. I pried four boys out of a dogpile on the floor, separated the girls who took turns pinching each other, and corralled the runners back into the corner by the door. The class formed a jagged, zigzagging line.

When the door to the playground opened, the class charged out, screaming. I didn't feel the usual urge to call them back, file them in a proper line, and make them try again. For the first time, I allowed them to scatter, unchecked. The sun blazed, searing my eyes. I had left my sunglasses inside. A child hurtled into my knees, knocking them together in a little embrace. Rylan pressed his face into the side of my thigh.

"Ms. Kathy?"

I grunted, counting kids on the playground, eyes scrunched against the sun.

"I like you. A lot."

"Sweetie, I—" He shot off, legs churning, toward the swings. "I like you, too."

About the Authors

Mijat Budimir Vujačić is an economist by trade and storyteller at heart. He has published three horror novels written in Serbian: *Krvavi Akvarel*, *NekRomansa*, and *Vampir*. His stories have appeared in *SQ*, *Encounters*, *Under the Bed*, and *Infernal Ink* magazines, as well as the anthologies *Silent Scream* and *The Nightmare Collective*. He believes a strong work ethic is the root of all success, and that it is best to err on the side of action. A fan of all things horror, he is also an avid gamer, hobby blogger, hookah enthusiast, and a devoted dog person. He lives in Belgrade, Serbia. You can email him at mbvujacic@gmail.com or follow him on Twitter @MBVujacic.

Robert Luke Wilkins was born in North East England and now makes his home in the mountains of California with his wife and two cats. He codes for a living, writes for pleasure, and plays too many games in his spare time. He can be found online at fatwriter.com, or on Twitter @RobertLWilkins.

Samuel Marzioli lives in Oregon with his family. His work has appeared in various publications, including *Apex Magazine*, *Intergalactic Medicine Show*, *Shock Totem*, and *Penumbra eMag*. For more information about his work, visit his website at marzioli.blogspot.com.

Erin Cole writes dark fiction from a small attic in Portland, Oregon. She is a member of the Horror Writers Association, won 10th place in the Writer's Digest 80th Annual Writing Competition and an

About the Authors

Honorable Mention in the 2009 Kay Snow Writing Contest, and has written works for more than 60 publications. When she's not reading or writing, she enjoys cooking, adopts rescue animals, and is pen pals with many things that go bump in the night. You can find her online at erincolewrites.com.

R. Y. Brockway writes short stories with the intent to entertain and thrill her readers. A lover of both the mundane and the macabre, she explores aspects of both in her writing. She lives with her husband in Virginia. You can find more of her work in *The Fiction Vortex*, *Fictionvale*, and *Every Day Fiction*.

Joshua Mannix lives in Columbus, Ohio where he writes fiction casually (for now) and works as a technical writer. He earned a degree in Creative Writing from Miami University and is a sponsor member of the Columbus Creative Cooperative, one of the main writing groups in the city. His website is joshmannix.wordpress.com, where he posts small articles about writing technique, tips, book reviews, and his own stories.

Loren Eaton lives in South Florida with his wife and children. He spends his days shuffling paper as a business manager, penning content for various freelance clients, and trying to convince his children that Clifford the Big Red Dog is a parable about the dangers of genetic engineering run amok. His fiction falls mostly in the dark fantasy, noir, and horror genres and has been published in a number of nice places such as *Needle: A Magazine of Noir*, *Port Iris*, *The Drabblecast*, and several anthologies. He blogs about narrative, genre, and the craft of writing at ISawLightningFall.com.

Sean Benham is a fresh, strange voice in fiction. Unafraid to delve into subjects that other authors would happily pass up, his work is both ethereal and deeply personal. He has a knack for creating alternate worlds that mirror our own in unfortunate ways, as well as the memorable characters who inhabit them. When he's not writing, Sean Benham is an entertainment industry professional who has worked as an art director, graphic animator, writer, and producer on everything from Emmy award-winning children's television programming to heavy metal music videos. He lives with his wife in Toronto.

Joshua Harding is a novelist, short story author, and award-winning poet and horror writer. He's worked as a nuclear missile mechanic, environmental lobbyist, cemetery restorer, freelance artist, puppet master, set designer, actor, carpenter, mortuary officer, and garbageman. The only career he's held longer than any of them is writer. His fiction has been featured in *Writer's Digest*, *QuarterReads*, and *The Loose Leaf Press*. He lives in a four-person artists' colony in the woods north of Chicago. You can follow Joshua on his website: jharding71.wix.com/joshuajharding.

Alicia Cusano-Weissenbach is an Italian-American writer who lives in Lawrence, Kansas with her husband, two cats, and a hamster. She works as an advocate for domestic violence survivors, and writes in her spare time. Her interest in writing began at a young age when she wrote stories like "The Coolest Horse" instead of going outside to play with other children.

M. James Bizzell currently lives in Houston, Texas where he splits his time between an attempt to complete a Master's degree in American Literature at Texas A&M University and staring at a keyboard until words show up on the adjoining screen. His reading and writing interests include all varieties of horror, from the meta to the Lovecraftian, dark and epic fantasy, and war stories both real and imagined. The author has recently started a website at writeyourwrongs.bizzell.biz where ideas and stories can be found, read, and reflected upon.

Dara Marquardt is a writer living in the High Rockies of Colorado. A complete list of her published works can be found at heartsintheattic.wordpress.com.

David Barclay currently lives in the greater San Francisco Bay Area with his wife Kristen. A game developer by day and author by night, he published his first novel, *The Aeschylus*, in December 2014. His other short fiction has appeared in *The Manor House* podcast and in the quarterly horror anthology *Infernal Ink*. He rambles about writing, film, and all things horror at david-barclay.com.

Kiya Krier recently abandoned her lucrative career as a preschool teacher to write short fiction full time. Now, making things up is called "paying the bills" instead of "lying." Kiya writes from whatever apartment in whatever city her husband, her bunny, and herself happen to reside. At the time of this publication, that city is Oceanside, California. She writes fiction in both realistic and speculative genres including but not limited to magical realism, fantasy, and science fiction. She can be found on her official website: kiyakrier.com.

About the Editor

Steven x Davis is a speculative fiction writer and freelance editor. He founded *Acidic Fiction* in 2014, editing and publishing 74 short stories and two anthologies before moving on to other projects. Steven also edited the English translations of two bestsellers for the Japanese government's Japan Library project: *Tree-Ring Management* and *Saving the Mill*. Steven published his debut fantasy novel, *Favor*, in February 2014 and is currently developing a picture book for children and robots. You can find many examples of his fiction and nonfiction writing at stevenxdavis.com.

www.ingramcontent.com/pod-product-compliance
Lightning Source LLC
Chambersburg PA
CBHW061213170626
46809CB00003B/1333